at war

Helen Peters

nosy crow

Also by

Helen Peters

FOR YOUNGER READERS

A Piglet Called Truffle
A Duckling Called Button
A Sheepdog Called Sky
A Kitten Called Holly
A Lamb Called Lucky
A Goat Called Willow
An Otter Called Pebble

FOR OLDER READERS

The Secret Hen House Theatre
The Farm Beneath the Water
Evie's Ghost

For all the children who have
had to leave their homes and make
new lives in other places

First published in the UK in 2019 by Nosy Crow Ltd
The Crow's Nest, 14 Baden Place
Crosby Row, London, SE1 1YW

www.nosycrow.com

ISBN: 978 1 78800 471 8

Printed and bound in Great Britain by Clays Ltd, Elcograf S.p.A.
Typeset by Tiger Media

Papers used by Nosy Crow are made from wood grown in
sustainable forests

1 3 5 7 9 10 8 6 4 2

CHAPTER ONE

A Letter From
the Secret Service

It was Mr Harte who started it all.

"We're going to be learning about World War Two," he told us on our first day in Year 6.

Everyone was excited, especially Jacob and Murphy, who actually cheered. They're obsessed with war, those two.

"Do any of you know anyone who lived through the Second World War?" Mr Harte asked.

I put my hand up, and so did a few other people. Mr Harte looked around the classroom and his eyes came to rest on me.

"Yes, Daniel?"

"My granny," I said. "She came over from Germany just before the war started."

"That's so interesting. Did your granny come to England as a refugee?"

"I think so," I said, feeling embarrassed now, because actually I wasn't sure. Granny didn't seem like a refugee to me.

Other people started asking questions.

"How old was she when she came to England?"

"I'm not sure."

"Was she a Nazi?"

"Of course she wasn't. She's really nice."

But that was the only thing I was sure about. The more questions they asked, the more I realised I didn't really know anything about Granny's childhood. I knew she left Germany to get away from Hitler, but anyone would want to get away from Hitler, wouldn't they? So I'd never asked any more questions. I'd always had the feeling that I shouldn't ask.

But now I really wanted to know more.

I decided to visit Granny on my way home. I often call in after school on a Wednesday. It's the only afternoon she isn't busy. Granny's eighty-nine years old, but she seems a lot younger.

"You have to keep active," she always says. "There's too much to do to sit around wasting time." So she goes on a two-mile walk with friends every morning, "to stop me seizing up". She also spends a lot of time working with a charity that helps refugees to settle in England, and she belongs to lots of clubs in the village, so she's hardly ever at home in the daytime.

I love going to Granny's. She's always pleased to see me and, as soon as I arrive, she puts the kettle on for tea and gets out the chocolate biscuits.

That afternoon was lovely and sunny, so we took the tea tray out to the garden table. As soon as Granny sat down, Inka, her black-and-white cat, jumped up on to her lap.

Inka came from a rescue centre, and she adores

Granny. I do like cats, but Inka is quite annoying. It would be fine if she just sat there, but instead she walks round and round on Granny's lap, miaowing really loudly, and then she starts clawing at Granny's clothes and sneezing all over her hands. I don't know how Granny stands it, but she's incredibly patient. She says Inka was probably taken away from her mother too early, so she has separation issues that make her needy and anxious.

I was waiting for Inka to settle down, and wondering how to bring up the topic of Granny's childhood, when she kind of did it for me.

"What are you doing at school at the moment?" she asked.

"We've just started learning about the Second World War," I said, taking a chocolate biscuit from the plate.

Granny reached for a teaspoon. "Oh?"

I took my chance.

"Mr Harte asked if any of us had relatives who were alive then. So I told him you came over from Germany just before the war."

Granny slowly stirred her tea. Her eyes were fixed on the blue and white mug.

"Everyone was really interested," I said. "They had lots of questions about it. But I didn't really know anything else."

Granny stayed silent for a minute. Then she said, "How strange that you should say that today."

"Is it? Why?"

"Such an odd coincidence."

"Why?" I asked again.

She raised her eyes from her mug and looked at me.

"I had a letter this morning. Completely out of the blue. From MI5."

I stared at her. "MI5? The spy agency?"

"That's right. The Secret Service. They're planning to release my Second World War files, and they're asking if I wish to remain anonymous or if I want to have my name and picture published."

I was baffled.

"Your Second World War files? Why does the Secret Service have files on you? You were only a child in the war, weren't you?"

"I was twelve when I came to England. But when all this happened, in 1940, I was thirteen."

"When what happened? When MI5 were spying on you? So did they spy on all Germans? Even children?"

Granny paused. "Not exactly." Then she gave me a mischievous, twinkly-eyed smile. "Well, not at all, in fact. No. They weren't spying on me."

"So why do they have files on you?"

Granny was silent for a very long time. Her eyes gazed across the garden, but she wasn't looking at the flowers, or the village street, or even the hills beyond. She was looking much further into the distance than that.

Just when I was beginning to think she might never speak again, she turned to look at me.

"Do you really want to know about it?"

"Yes," I said. "I really do."

Granny looked at me thoughtfully. "It feels right that I should tell you now, when you're almost the same age as I was when it all started."

"So what happened?" I asked impatiently.

She smiled. "I need to find some things first. Can you wait a few days?"

"Sure," I said, though I was a bit disappointed. I was bursting with curiosity since she'd mentioned MI5.

"How about Sunday? I should be ready by then."

Ready for what? I wondered. But I didn't ask any more questions. We talked about other things until I'd finished all the biscuits and it was time to go home.

When I went round to Granny's on Sunday, there was a box I hadn't seen before lying open on the living-room table. There were lots of old letters in it, and a faded notebook. Next to the box sat a framed black-and-white photo of a man in a shirt and trousers, and a woman in a flower-patterned dress. They both had kind, gentle faces. He had his arm around her shoulders and they were smiling at the camera.

I had seen the photo before. It normally sat on Granny's bedside table. Once, when I was younger, I asked her who the people were. She said they were her parents, but there was something in the way she said it that meant I didn't ask any more questions.

I had no idea what to expect when I sat down with Granny that afternoon, armed with Mum's phone to record our conversation.

I certainly didn't expect the story I heard. And I also didn't expect it to give me an idea for Granny's ninetieth birthday present.

Mum had been worrying about what to get Granny for her ninetieth birthday. There didn't seem to be anything she really wanted. But Granny's story gave me an idea. The best idea for a present I've ever had.

Granny seemed to take longer than usual making the tea that day. When I carried in the tray and we sat down, she told me she had never really talked about her childhood before. Not even to her own children. Some parts of it had been too painful to remember, she said. Other parts had been top secret.

"But now I want you to hear it. There aren't too many of us left, and it would be a shame if our stories died with us."

So here it is, in her own words. The extraordinary wartime story of my grandmother, Anna Schlesinger.

CHAPTER TWO

Open Up!

I shall never forget the night my life changed forever. It was the ninth of November, 1938, and Uncle Paul had come for supper.

They thought I was in bed, but I wasn't. I was sitting on the hall floor, leaning against the living-room door, listening to every word they said.

Listening at the door was the only way to find out what was really going on. These days, my parents' conversations always seemed to stop when I came into the room. I knew they were trying to protect me from the truth. As if that was possible.

So all through our supper with Uncle Paul, we talked cheerfully about nothing in particular. It was only now, after they had sent me off to bed, that they would speak honestly about the situation.

Uncle Paul was my favourite relative after Mama and Papa. He was Mama's younger brother, and he was one of those people who could make everything fun, even something completely normal, like a walk to the shops. My parents were quite serious, so I always loved spending time with Paul.

But now, even Paul was leaving me. He was a

doctor, but Hitler had said Jewish doctors weren't allowed to treat non-Jews. Since there were hardly any Jewish families in our little town, Paul couldn't afford to live here any more. And he had friends in Paris who said they could find him work there.

Even though I knew this, I was angry with him for deserting me. Everything in my world seemed to be falling apart. School was awful. The other children didn't speak to me any more. Even my best friend Ingrid, who lived across the street, had stopped coming round to play.

"So that's it," said Mama. I heard the rattle of the coffee cups as she put them on the table. "Once you go tomorrow, we'll be the only members of the family still in Germany."

"And you need to get out too," said Paul. "When are you going to wake up? You're like ostriches, the pair of you, with your heads buried in the sand. You're intelligent people, for goodness' sake. I don't understand it."

"We're not free-and-easy youngsters like you," said Papa. "We can't just get on a train with a rucksack on our backs. Where would we go? What would we do? I don't want my family to be refugees in a foreign country, with no money and nowhere to live. I'm too old to start again. And how would I find work in a country where I don't even speak the language?"

"Hans and Ruth found work in England," said Paul.

"As servants! And then only because that cousin

of Ruth's in Manchester begged a favour from her rich neighbour. And Hans is a professor of law!"

"*Was* a professor of law," said Uncle Paul, "until the Nazis took away his job."

"He's never even picked up a spade," said Mama. "How on earth is he going to work as a gardener? With his bad back too. And Ruth employed as a cook, when she's never made a meal in her life. They'll be fired within a week, and then they'll be homeless in a foreign country. What will happen to them then?"

"At least they won't be here," said Uncle Paul. "That's the only thing that matters now."

"It was different for them," said Papa. "Hans can't work here any more. But I have my own business."

I heard Uncle Paul groan in frustration. "The Nazis are taking away Jewish businesses every day. You know what happened to Alfred's shop. What makes you think you're special?"

"Shops, yes," said Papa, "but we're a highly respected publishing house. The business has been in the family for three generations. They can't take that away."

"They can do whatever they want, and nobody lifts a finger to stop them. All the Polish Jews have already been deported. I don't know why you think they won't touch you."

"We're not Polish," said Papa. "We're German. We've been German for generations."

"And you're Jewish," said Paul.

"But we're not even religious," said Mama.

9

Uncle Paul gave a bitter laugh. "And you think that will save you? You think Hitler's thugs will spare you because you don't go to synagogue? You're a pair of idiots."

My father never shouted. He went dangerously quiet instead. His voice was very quiet now.

"That's enough, Paul," he said. "You'll wake Anna."

I tensed, ready for a silent sprint to my room in case somebody decided to come and check on me. But it didn't seem as though anyone was going to move. My mother spoke in a strained, quavery voice.

"Walter is a war hero. He won the Iron Cross. Even Hitler isn't going to turn on war veterans."

"I don't understand you," said Paul, and his voice was quiet and despairing now. "You do listen to the radio, don't you? You have heard his speeches?"

I had heard his speeches, although my parents didn't know that. They turned off the radio if I came into the room when he was speaking. So I listened from the hall instead.

Hitler never seemed to speak in a normal voice. He shouted and screamed, and he sounded completely mad. It was really frightening, especially when he ranted and raved about how the Jews were responsible for all the problems in Germany.

I couldn't make sense of the world any more. Why was it such a terrible thing to be Jewish?

I tensed up. Harsh voices were shouting in the street. I heard glass smashing and then boots clattering down the road.

"There," said Paul. "That's your friendly, understanding Nazis, just having a bit of fun."

"Let's not argue any more," said Mama. "This is the last time we'll see you for who knows how long. Are you really taking Mitzi to France with you?"

Mitzi was Paul's cat, a big, fluffy, black-and-white beauty. Paul adored her.

"Of course I am," he said. "She likes train journeys. She'll be happy in her basket."

"Let's have some music," said Papa.

That was one of his favourite sentences. It was the cue for Mama to sit at the beautiful grand piano. Sometimes, if it was earlier in the evening, they would ask me to play for them too.

The dining chairs scraped back across the polished floor. I tried to spring to my feet, but my legs were stiff from crouching and I nearly fell over. I managed to steady myself and pad across the hall to my bedroom.

I lay awake for a while, listening to the music. It must have lulled me to sleep, because the next thing I remember is waking with a violent lurch of the stomach. Somebody was thumping on the front door of our apartment, and a man's voice shouted, "Open up! Open up now!"

CHAPTER THREE

The Night
of Broken Glass

"Open up!" barked the voice again.

Something heavy smashed against the front door.

My bedroom door creaked open. My stomach knotted in terror.

"Anna," whispered Mama, pulling back the bedclothes. "Get in the wardrobe, quick."

More smashing on the door, and men's voices swearing.

"What's happening?" I tried to say, but my throat was closed up and no words came out.

"In the wardrobe," Mama whispered urgently. She was half-pushing, half-carrying me across the room. She swept the clothes to one side and bundled me into the wardrobe, pulling the hangers back across so the clothes hid me. It was even darker than the room. My heart hammered in my chest.

Another tremendous smash. Harsh voices shouting inside our apartment.

Was that Papa's voice speaking to them? It was hard to tell over the shouting.

Where was Mama? Was she hiding, too?

More smashing and crashing. It sounded like

china and glass.

A scream. Mama!

Her scream stopped abruptly, as though someone had clapped a hand over her mouth. Glass shattered; crockery smashed; men shouted; doors banged; piano keys crashed; wood cracked and splintered.

My bedroom door opened. Light appeared around the edges of the wardrobe doors. Someone had switched the light on. Who?

Smashing, tearing, stabbing.

With trembling hands, I parted the dresses and peeped through the narrow gap between the wardrobe doors.

No!

Two Nazi storm troopers were destroying my room. One man stabbed through my bedclothes with a bayonet, slashing at the mattress and the pillow. I turned ice-cold. Would he have done that if I had still been in the bed?

The other one had an axe. He pulled out the drawers from my chest of drawers and tipped my clothes all over the floor. Then he swung his axe up high and brought it down on one of the drawers over and over again, smashing it to pieces.

Over there was my bookcase, filled with picture books I'd had since I was a baby and storybooks I read again and again. Would he destroy them next? Or would he come for the wardrobe?

The other man was slashing my bedclothes to shreds.

Oh, no!

I almost let out a shriek, but I clamped my mouth shut just in time.

Alfred, the teddy bear I'd slept with every night of my life, lay in the bed right next to my pillow.

Leave him alone, I silently screamed. *Leave him alone!*

The man with the axe kicked the final drawer hard with his shiny boot. The sides collapsed on to the floor. He turned to face the wardrobe.

I stopped breathing. I shrank back, pressing myself against the wood.

A scream. A wild, unearthly scream.

I looked through the crack in the doors. Mama ran into the room, her hair dishevelled, her face bright red and distorted with fear and rage. She shoved the man aside and sprang to the wardrobe, pressing herself in front of it, blocking my view.

"Leave it!" she cried. "Leave it alone! There's a child in there."

I heard a scuffle and my mother's cry as the man pushed her aside. The wardrobe doors were wrenched open. He grabbed my arm and yanked me out. Mama pulled me away from him and dragged me into the hall.

"Put your shoes on. Quick," she whispered.

I stuffed my feet into my shoes. I heard the men hacking the wardrobe to pieces. Mama grabbed our coats and we hurried out, stepping over the splinters of our smashed front door.

"Where's Papa?" I asked, as we ran down the stairs. "Why isn't he coming?"

Mama didn't answer. A sick, cold feeling settled in my stomach.

"Mama? Where is he?"

She gripped my hand tighter. At the bottom of the stairs, she led me to the back door that opened into the shared garden of our apartment block. She unlocked the door and we ran to the garden shed. Mama pulled me inside and shut the door behind us. She cleared a space among the tools on the floor and we sat down, our backs against the wall. My heart was thumping against my ribs.

"What if they find us here?" I said.

Mama didn't answer. She just hugged me tight.

I heard glass smashing on the street, and the tramping of boots in the road behind our garden. What would happen if they burst into the shed? I couldn't think about that. I screwed my eyes shut. The world behind my eyelids flashed red and black with terror.

"Where's Papa?" I said, through my half-closed throat. "Is he...?"

I couldn't say the word, but she knew what I meant.

"No," she said. "No, Anna. He's just had to go away for a while, that's all."

"They took him away?"

"Yes." I could tell she was trying not to cry.

"Where?"

She shook her head. "I don't know. We'll find out. Don't worry, darling."

How could she tell me not to worry?

We sat there in silence, listening to tramping boots, shouting and destruction. I tried just to listen and not to think. I couldn't let myself think.

Eventually the boots faded into the distance. "Come on," said Mama. "Let's go indoors."

"No!" I said, a picture of our shattered apartment flooding my mind's eye. "I'm not going back."

Mama took a deep breath. "Where else would we go?"

"What if they're lying in wait for us?"

"They've all gone now. And maybe Papa's back."

I hadn't thought of that. If Papa came home and found the apartment empty, he would be so worried.

I could hardly stand up, I was so stiff from the cold and sitting for hours on the floor.

When we got into the apartment, I called, "Papa! Papa!"

No reply. Where was he? What were they doing to him?

Panic overwhelmed me. My throat closed up and I thought I was going to choke. Mama put her arms around me.

"Stay strong, Anna," she said. "We must stay strong for Papa. You need to sleep now."

I refused to go to bed until we'd searched the whole apartment. Shards of glass from picture frames and ornaments crunched beneath our shoes. The piano was smashed to splinters. The kitchen floor was littered with pieces of Mama's wedding china. But there was nobody there. And they hadn't hurt Alfred. They had knocked my bookcase to the floor, but they hadn't actually destroyed the books. I set the bookcase upright and started to put the poor books back.

"You need to go to bed, Anna," said Mama. "You can sleep in my room."

"I have to put these back first," I said, panic rising inside me. I couldn't bear to see them spilled all over the floor like that, with their spines cracked and their pages splayed and crumpled. "I have to put them back."

So Mama knelt beside me and we put all the books back on the shelves. Then we both got into her bed, which hadn't been attacked like mine.

I was certain I wouldn't be able to sleep, but the bed was so soft, and I was suddenly so overcome with exhaustion, that the next thing I knew I was waking up to the sound of birds singing outside the window. I had a few untroubled seconds before I remembered, and my stomach contracted so violently that I had to run to the bathroom.

The bathroom looked just as it always had. It was the one room the Nazis had left alone.

CHAPTER FOUR

What About Mitzi?

The next morning Frau Gumpert, my former best friend Ingrid's mother, came to see us. When she saw the state of the apartment, she burst into tears.

"I'm so ashamed. I'm so ashamed to be German. I don't know what's happened to my country."

Mama tried to comfort her. "It's not your fault. And you shouldn't be here. I don't want to put your family in danger."

But Frau Gumpert only went home to fetch some of her cups and plates, and bring us bread and coffee. Then she insisted on staying all day to clean up the apartment, so Mama could spend the time making phone calls to find out where Papa was.

Herr Pulver, from the apartment above ours, also came to see us. He apologised for not doing anything to help during the night.

"I'm a coward. I was too afraid of what they'd do to my family if I tried to stop them."

"Of course," said Mama. "It's not your fault. You can't put your family in danger."

"How can I help?" he asked. "What do you need?"

"There's no need," said Mama. "You mustn't take

18

risks for us."

But he was desperate to do something, so Mama asked him to repair the front door. Herr Pulver hurried off to fetch tools and wood. It soon became clear that he was no carpenter. After several hours of sawing and hammering, the mended door looked like very bad patchwork, but at least it had no holes in it. He fixed a padlock on the outside and bolts on the inside.

"Thank you very much," said Mama. "It's good to know we'll be safe now."

We all looked at the door. And I knew, with a certainty that came like a blow to the stomach, that the strongest door in the world would be no use at all any more.

After hours on the phone, Mama discovered that Papa had been taken to a concentration camp called Buchenwald. I had heard of concentration camps. They were prisons for people the Nazis didn't like.

"He'll be back soon," Mama said. Her hands were shaking.

"When?" I asked.

"Soon."

"But you don't know that, do you? What if he doesn't come back?"

Mama looked stricken, and I felt bad for saying it. But I was angry too. She shouldn't say things if they weren't true.

At five o'clock Frau Gumpert went home to cook

supper for her family. She came back in the evening and told us there had been attacks on Jews all over Germany and Austria last night. Thirty thousand Jewish men had been taken to concentration camps. Almost every synagogue and thousands of Jewish homes and businesses were destroyed.

The Nazis said they had done this in revenge for a Jewish man shooting a Nazi official in Paris.

It became known as *Kristallnacht*. The Night of Broken Glass.

The next day Mama found out that Uncle Paul had also been taken to Buchenwald. It sounds awful, but at first I actually felt glad. At least he would be with Papa. At least they'd have each other.

Then I felt dreadful. Poor, poor Uncle Paul. Now he wouldn't be able to go to Paris.

Suddenly a terrible picture flashed into my head.

"What about Mitzi? We have to go and find her."

"We will," said Mama. "Later."

"Not later! Now! What if they hurt her? What if she's trapped under something? We have to go now."

Mama looked at me. "All right. We'll fetch her now."

Uncle Paul lived in a sunny, high-ceilinged apartment on the main street, next to Herr and Frau Heinkel's drapery store. The Heinkels had had that store since Mama was a child. Mama always took me there to buy coats and shoes and dress material. I loved choosing the fabric for my summer dresses from the rolls of pretty cottons.

As we walked up the street, I gasped and grabbed Mama's arm.

"Look!"

The windows of the Heinkels' store were smashed to pieces. All that was left were a few jagged shards around the edges. Inside, the shelves had been pulled off the walls and the shop was completely bare except for torn scraps of paper and trampled ends of ribbons on the floor.

As we stared in horror, the door from the back storeroom opened and Frau Heinkel came out. She looked frail and old. She stared blankly for a moment before she recognised us and attempted a watery smile.

Mama stepped through the hole where the plate-glass window had been and hugged her.

"I'm so sorry, Vera. I'm so sorry. Where's Manfred? Did they take him?"

Frau Heinkel nodded. "Did they take Walter?"

Mama nodded too. Then she looked at Frau Heinkel's wrinkled hands, which were criss-crossed with little red cuts and scratches.

"Oh, Vera, what did they do to you?"

"After they'd destroyed the shop," Frau Heinkel said, "they ordered me to clear up all the mess. There was so much broken glass."

"Did they steal all your stock too?"

Frau Heinkel shook her head. In a small, tired voice, she said, "Our neighbours came and looted it all. The police stood by and watched them. All our customers. Half those people, Manfred's been giving them credit for years. I suppose they thought they could just help themselves to the rest."

Mama's eyes were filled with tears. "I'm so sorry, Vera. It's just terrible. Where are you going to go? You can't stay here on your own. Do you want to come and stay with us?"

"That's very kind, Edith, but I'm going to stay with my daughter in Frankfurt tomorrow. She's trying to get us all visas to go to Palestine. Where are you going to go?"

Mama shook her head. "I don't know. I don't know anything any more."

"You have to get out," said Frau Heinkel. "You know that, don't you? You must get out."

Mama nodded slowly. "We didn't want to leave. Walter was so sure things would get better. But now..."

She left the sentence unfinished, and she and Frau Heinkel said a tearful goodbye.

"We won't leave before Papa gets back, will we?" I asked, as we stopped in front of Uncle Paul's apartment block. "We'll wait for Papa?"

"Of course," said Mama.

Always before, as our friends and family had emigrated one by one, I'd been glad we were staying. I didn't want to leave our lovely apartment, with my cosy bedroom and all my precious things. But now, all I felt was relief. It was obvious we couldn't stay any more.

I wondered where we'd go. I hoped it would be England. I had seen the pictures of King George VI's coronation in the magazines and newspapers. The king and queen and the little princesses had looked so splendid in their jewels and cloaks. It seemed like a different world.

Mama had brought her set of keys, but Uncle Paul's apartment was unlocked. The front door wasn't damaged though. Maybe he'd let the storm troopers in before they smashed the door down.

I was terrified of what we might find, but the apartment hadn't been destroyed as badly as ours. Cupboards had been opened and ransacked, and all the papers pulled out of Paul's desk, but the furniture was still intact.

To my joy and relief, Mitzi was curled up in her usual spot on the window seat. I gave her a big cuddle before I went to fetch her wicker basket from the kitchen.

As I crossed the hall, there was a sharp knock at the door. We froze. The contents of my stomach turned to water.

"*Heil Hitler!*" barked an unknown voice. The door opened and an SS officer stepped into the hall, in black uniform with gleaming buttons and boots. He frowned at Mama. My teeth started to chatter. I tried to clamp my mouth shut but I couldn't control it.

"This is not your apartment, I believe," he said.

Mama had turned very pale. "It belongs to my brother."

"My commanding officer needs this apartment. He will be taking possession of it tomorrow morning.

Give me the key."

"But what about my brother's things?"

"You will leave everything as it is. Take nothing with you. Give me the key. That is an order."

Without a word, my mother handed the front door key to him. He turned it over in his palm, then tried it in the lock. Once he was sure it was the right key, he thrust out his arm again, said, "*Heil Hitler!*" and ordered us to leave.

"I have to get Mitzi," I said.

My mother shot a terrified glance at the officer. He said nothing. I went into the living room and scooped Mitzi's warm, furry body up from the window seat. Mitzi liked being cuddled and she snuggled happily into my arms.

"Aren't you a beautiful cat?" the officer said, in a soppy voice, as I carried her through the hall to the kitchen.

He reached out and stroked her. Was he going to take Mitzi too? I tightened my hold on her. If Paul came back and found her gone, it would break his heart. I put her in the basket and fastened the straps around the lid. Mitzi hated going in the basket. She started to yowl.

"Shh, be quiet," I whispered. "You won't be in there for long."

I remembered that Paul always put food in the basket to keep her quiet. Too late now. I had to get her out before the officer ordered me to leave her behind.

I held my breath as I carried her through the hall.

But the man said nothing. He waited for Mama and me to leave the apartment, and then he locked the door behind us and pocketed the key.

CHAPTER FIVE

Jews Are
Not Wanted

I was nervous and jumpy all the time now. What made it worse was that I could tell Mama was frightened too. She tried to pretend everything was fine, but she jumped whenever the phone rang or there was a knock at the door.

It was worse, too, because I couldn't go to school any more. Jewish children were now banned from German schools, and the nearest Jewish school had been burned down on Kristallnacht. So I had to stay at home all day. We only went out to buy food and essentials. I insisted on going with Mama every time she left the apartment, even if she was just going to buy bread. I knew it wasn't logical, but somehow I felt she would be safer if I was with her.

But Mama had a great idea.

"Let's learn English," she said. "We can surprise Papa by speaking perfect English to him when he gets back."

"When he gets back" was a phrase we both used a lot at that time. I had trained myself not to think about what might be happening to Papa. It felt as though I had a little box inside my head, where I locked away all the things I didn't allow myself to think about.

We had learned a little bit of English at school. But when Mama was a child, her parents had wanted her to learn the language, so she'd had an English nanny for a while, and she had kept all her English workbooks.

My new best friends were two little leather-bound pocket dictionaries: a red one, which was German to English, and a blue one for English to German. I became completely absorbed. When I was learning English I could forget about the horrible world outside, sometimes for hours at a time. I made Mama test me on my vocabulary and at mealtimes we would try to speak in English. She had forgotten a lot, but it came back to her quite quickly, and she could correct my pronunciation.

Learning English and having Mitzi to keep me company made my new life indoors more bearable. In any case, even if we had gone outdoors, there was barely anywhere we could go. Jews were banned from parks, swimming pools, theatres, cinemas and ice rinks. The notices were everywhere: *Juden Sind Unerwünscht*. Jews Are Not Wanted.

Then, three weeks later, I woke one morning and heard a man's voice in the apartment. My stomach clenched. Rigid with terror, I listened.

It wasn't shouting. It was a quiet voice. It sounded like…

No. It couldn't be.

Could it?

A gentle knock at my door.

"Anna?" my mother called softly.

I sat up in bed, holding my breath.

The door opened. A figure stood in the shadowy doorway.

"Papa! Oh, Papa!"

I leapt into his arms and hugged him and hugged him. He hugged me back tightly and I laid my head on his chest, flooded with happiness.

But when we finally let each other go and I stepped back and saw him properly, I was shocked.

He looked stooped and thin and much, much older. He had bruises and cuts on his face, and he wasn't wearing his glasses. His hair was greyer and thinner and his hands trembled.

"Oh, Anna, it's so good to see you. You look so well. I'm sure you've grown."

"Sit down, Walter," said Mama gently, and we all sat on the bed, Mama and I on either side of Papa. He put an arm around each of us and we snuggled up together, my head on his shoulder.

"It's so wonderful to be back with my girls. I've missed you so much."

"You're so skinny," I said. "What did they do to you?"

He shook his head quickly, as though trying to dislodge the memories. "Let's not talk about that. Tell me all about you."

"But—"

He took my face in his wrinkled, shaking hands. They were like the hands of an old, old man.

"No more questions, Anna."

"But—"

Mama gave me a warning look. "Anna, you mustn't ask. Really. They told Papa that if he says anything about what happened there, they'll come and get him again."

I turned cold. What had they done to him? What must his life have been like in that camp?

"Anyway," said Papa, "now that I'm back, I just want to hear about you. Tell me what you've been up to."

He was clearly making a huge effort to seem normal. If he could be that brave, after a month in a concentration camp, then there was no excuse for me not to be brave too.

"We have Mitzi now," I said. "We went to Uncle Paul's flat and fetched her. I made her a toy from a cork tied to a piece of wool and she loves it. When I pull it around the apartment she chases it and pounces on it like it's a mouse."

"That's good," he said. "Paul will be pleased."

"Did you—" I began, and then I stopped. I had been going to ask him whether he'd seen Uncle Paul in Buchenwald.

"Mama says you're learning English," Papa said. And, relieved to have found a safer topic, I told him about the irregular verbs I'd learned yesterday.

CHAPTER SIX

Anna Must Go

A few days later, Uncle Paul came out of Buchenwald too. Since the Nazis had taken his home, he came to live with us until he could get to France. His emigration papers had expired while he was in the concentration camp, so he had to go to the consulates every day to try to get the necessary permissions again.

Papa couldn't go back to work. While he was in Buchenwald, the Nazis took his publishing company. They made a law that all Jewish businesses had to be transferred to non-Jewish owners.

Now it wasn't only Uncle Paul telling him we had to get out of Germany. Everyone we knew told us to leave. And Papa, who looked older and sadder every day, finally agreed. He left the apartment each morning at the same time as before, but instead of going to his office he and Uncle Paul spent every day in queues at the foreign consulates, trying to get the right papers to go to America, Holland or England. But every week the Nazis were making new rules about emigration, and each new law meant new documents were needed. You had to have several different documents before they would let you leave, and each one was only valid for a short time, so it was very difficult to have all the right papers at once. Every day, Papa and Uncle Paul came home looking more tired and more defeated.

One Monday morning, in April 1939, while Papa was out, a letter arrived for Mama. She took it to the kitchen and sat at the table, where I was learning English vocabulary. The kitchen table was one of the only pieces of furniture we had left after Kristallnacht.

I glanced at Mama as she read the letter. She was whiter than I had ever seen her.

"Who's it from?" I asked.

She didn't answer. Her hands shook as she put the letter back in the envelope and tucked it in her apron pocket. I didn't ask her again. I was too scared of what the answer might be.

All day, my stomach was knotted with worry. I tried to work on my English, but I couldn't concentrate. I tried to read a book, but I couldn't take in the words. I did some drawing, but it didn't take my mind off the letter. What did it say? Were they going to take Papa away again? Were they going to take us all away?

Papa came home in the afternoon, tired and preoccupied. Paul had gone to visit a friend. Mama made my favourite supper of little sausages and potato salad. It was her favourite supper too, but that evening she hardly ate any of it. Her face was strained and she just pushed the food around the plate. Papa barely spoke, and he didn't seem to notice how tense Mama was. Their quietness paralysed me into silence, too. The meal seemed to last forever.

Eventually, when Papa and I had finished eating, Mama looked up from her plate.

"I had a letter today," she said.

I stopped breathing. Papa looked up expectantly. Mama took a long quavery breath.

"There's a place for Anna on a children's transport going to England."

I stared at her. "For me?"

She nodded.

"Just me? On my own? Without you?"

Mama nodded again. My insides felt as though they had been scooped out.

"No. I'm not going on my own. I can't go without you."

I turned to Papa. He had gone completely white.

"I can't, can I, Papa? Tell Mama I can't go."

Papa said nothing. I felt hollow.

Mama's hands were gripping the table. "It's only for a little while. It will give me and Papa time to get everything sorted out here, and then we can come and join you."

"But why can't we all go together? What's a children's transport, anyway?"

"Frau Heinkel told me about it." Her voice was strained and her eyes didn't meet mine. "People are organising trains to take Jewish children to England, to live with foster families. I put your name on the list. I didn't tell you because I didn't think you'd get a place. But I heard this morning that you have, and there's a kind family in England who have offered to take you in."

"But I don't want to live with another family!"

"It's just for a short time. Until we get our papers. They're making it easier for children to get papers, you see, so you can go first. As soon as we can, we'll come and join you."

"With the same family?"

"If we can, yes. Or close by, anyway."

Suddenly I had an idea that filled me with relief.

"I can find work for you!"

If I could do a useful job, then there was some sense in my going to England before them.

"When I get to England, I'll ask everybody I meet, and I'll find jobs for both of you."

I expected Papa to object, but he just sat with his head bowed so I couldn't see his expression. Mama gave me a tight smile. Her cheeks were flushed and she looked feverish.

I couldn't bear the silence.

"When am I leaving?"

Mama hesitated and glanced at Papa. When she spoke, her voice was choked.

"Wednesday."

I stared at her. "Next Wednesday? In six days?"

Mama nodded. I had that hollowed-out feeling again.

"Who are the family? What are they like? What if they don't like me?"

"Of course they'll like you," said Mama. She tried

to turn her strained expression into a smile. "Who could help liking you?"

I thought of everyone at school turning their backs when I tried to talk to them.

"But who are they?" I asked. "Are they Jewish?"

"I don't know anything about them," said Mama, "but I know they'll be good people. The British government has agreed to take in Jewish children, to keep them safe, and kind people all over Britain have volunteered to be foster parents."

I said nothing. Why couldn't we be safe in our own country? Why should we have to leave our home? My hatred for Hitler surged up so violently that I wanted to hit something.

"Walter?" said Mama. "Are you all right? What do you think?"

Papa's face was tight and tense, and frighteningly white. His eyes were shining with unshed tears. I turned cold with shock. I had never seen him cry.

He swallowed and nodded. When he spoke, his voice was quiet and flat.

"Yes," he said. "Anna must go."

CHAPTER SEVEN

One Small Suitcase

Children travelling on the *Kindertransport* were allowed to take one small suitcase each. We all had to carry our own cases, so they couldn't be too heavy. We weren't allowed to take anything valuable out of the country, and only ten marks each in money.

Mama paid Frau Heinkel to make new dresses for me, some in my size and some bigger, in case I grew quickly. They were lovely dresses. Mama embroidered my name in all of them. I tried to imagine myself wearing them in England.

I didn't even know which part of Britain my foster family lived in. Would I be walking by the River Thames in London wearing that wool dress, gazing up at Big Ben and the Houses of Parliament? Or would I be high up in the Scottish mountains?

Maybe they lived by the sea. I had never seen the sea, but now I would be crossing it to get to England. Every day I traced the journey on the map in my children's atlas. Across Germany to the Dutch border, then through Holland to the English Channel, and over the sea to the port of Harwich, on the east coast of England. And from there to an unknown family.

At night, I lay in bed trying to imagine every possible type of family, so I would be prepared for whoever I ended up with. I imagined old parents and young ones; city families and country families; rich and poor; good-looking and ugly; parents with babies and parents with teenagers; families with one child and families with ten.

What if they weren't nice to me? What if they were mean, cruel people?

But they wouldn't be, would they? If they had offered to take in a refugee child, they must be good and kind.

Once my clothes and shoes were packed, there wasn't much room for anything else.

"Just one toy and one book, I'm afraid," said Mama. "When we come to join you, we can bring some more. And we'll pack up everything else carefully and leave it with friends until we get back."

It wasn't hard to decide which toy to take. There was no way I could have left Alfred behind. He had shared my bed for my whole life. Having him with me would be almost like travelling with a friend.

It was horrible to have to leave all the others behind though. Even though a lot of my toys were too young for me now, I didn't want to be parted from them. Papa said the foster family would probably have things I could play with, but that wasn't really the point. And anyway, what if they didn't want me playing with their things?

But I didn't say that aloud.

The worst thing was choosing which book to take. How could I possibly decide?

It seemed more sensible to take one I hadn't read yet, but that was such a risk. What if it wasn't any good? Then my only book would be one I didn't even like.

In the end, I decided on *Heidi*. I loved that book and I knew it would be a comfort. After all, Heidi also had to leave her home to live with people she'd never met, and everything worked out well in the end.

"As soon as we have your address, we can send you some more books," Mama said. "You can write and tell us which you'd like."

"But what if the Nazis don't let you send them?"

"I'm sure they won't make a fuss about a few books," she said.

I didn't believe her. It was obvious that the Nazis didn't want us to have anything at all. Why would they let me have my books?

The train was due to leave at midnight on Wednesday. I normally had to go to bed at nine, so, despite the strangeness of everything, it felt quite exciting to be up so late. Mama made my favourite supper again. Uncle Paul was very jolly.

"I expect the king and queen will be there to welcome you," he said. "Be sure to curtsy nicely, and then you might get invited to tea with the princesses."

Mama insisted on doing one last check of my suitcase, even though we had checked and packed it a hundred times. She slipped in a photograph of her and Papa, and then she put my writing case on top of everything else. "It will remind you to write to us as soon as you get there. You can write on the train, and then the minute you arrive in England you can post the letter, and we'll know you've arrived safely. Promise you'll do that."

I promised. And then I tucked a little bundle of drawing pencils between my folded clothes.

Mama and Papa were so worried about being late that we set off hours early. The train was leaving from Frankfurt, so we had to take a bus to the city. It wasn't cold outside, but to save room in my suitcase I was wearing my winter coat, hat and scarf, as well as several layers of clothing, so I was hot and sticky and really uncomfortable.

The whole way to Frankfurt, Mama and Papa each held one of my hands. Mama's hand clutched mine so tightly I was worried she would crush my bones.

When we got to the station, Papa carried my case, and in her free hand Mama held a paper bag full of food for the journey. We had to bring enough food to last until we got to England.

Even though we were early, the platform was already packed with parents and children. SS men were striding about, keeping an eye on everyone, shouting at people and sometimes hitting somebody just for fun. Some children were crying. Much worse, some parents were crying.

"Don't cry, will you?" I said to Mama. I could be brave as long as my parents were.

Mama flashed me a smile. "Of course not." She seemed all right, but her face was very red and, when I kissed her, her cheeks were boiling hot.

"You will come soon, won't you?" I said.

"Very soon, God willing."

Those last two words sent a chill through me. What did that mean?

I locked the thought away in the box inside my head.

CHAPTER EIGHT

Try to
Be Happy

We had to line up on the platform. My parents stood in line with me, still gripping my hands. A kind-looking man who wasn't in uniform started calling out our names.

I waited and waited. Almost all the children were on the train now. Had there been some terrible mistake? Maybe I wasn't on the list after all.

I was sure my parents were having the same worry, because they stopped talking and just stared, as rigid as statues, at the man calling out the names. I was so tense I could hardly breathe.

I realised, to my surprise, that I would be devastated if I couldn't leave on this train. I had to get to England. I had to find jobs for my parents so they could get out too.

"Anna Schlesinger?" the man called.

I felt dizzy with relief. Dragging my parents behind me, I went to the table where the man was sitting. A lady hung a cardboard label with a number on it on a piece of string around my neck. Another lady tied a label with the same number to my suitcase.

"You can get on the train now," she said.

Now I was worried I'd start crying. I bit my cheeks. I didn't dare look my parents in the eye. They were gripping my hands even more tightly than before.

Together, we walked towards the train. As we were about to board it, an SS officer stepped in front of us.

"No adults on the train!" he barked.

Mama pulled me into her coat and hugged me fiercely. Then Papa did the same. The rough wool felt scratchy against my face. My cheek was crushed against his top button. He lifted me up and kissed me, and Mama put her arms around both of us, and she stood on tiptoe and kissed me too. Then Papa put me down and handed me my suitcase. He kissed me again and said, "You'd better get on the train."

"We'll see you soon, darling," said Mama. "Be a good, helpful girl to your foster parents. We'll all be together again soon."

"You must be my brave, cheerful daughter," said Papa. "And we'll come and join you, as soon as we've got everything sorted out."

As I was about to climb the steps, Mama clutched my hand again.

"Try to be happy," she said. "Always be kind. And make the most of every opportunity you get. Fill your head with good things. And remember, we'll be thinking of you and sending our love to you every moment of every day."

I nodded, but I couldn't speak for the lump in my throat, and I didn't dare look at them in case it made me cry.

A man called, "Everybody on the train now!"

I wriggled my hand out of Mama's grip and climbed up the steps. "Write to us," she called. "Write to us as soon as you get there."

I nodded again, but I didn't trust myself to turn and look at them. I walked into the train corridor.

A lady with a list checked my number and showed me into a compartment. She put my case on the luggage rack.

The children in the compartment were jostling at the open window, calling and waving to their parents. Some of them were sobbing.

I hadn't said goodbye! I hadn't even looked at my parents. I had to see them and say goodbye properly. I had to smile and wave and show them I was all right.

I leaned over the smaller children and frantically scanned the crowd. Where were they? I tried to arrange my face into a smile, in case they were looking at me.

The soldiers started pushing all the parents away from the platform. One mother was crying hysterically, trying to get to the train. A soldier yelled at her but she took no notice. He slapped her in the face and she fell to the ground. Other parents helped her up.

Papa! There he was, helping her, comforting her. And there was Mama next to him, scooping up the handbag the woman had dropped, saving it from being crushed by the throng.

The whistle blew. Steam hissed. My parents looked

up and finally I caught their eyes. They smiled and waved and blew me kisses, and I waved and smiled and blew kisses back to them.

The train started to move out of the station. A soldier was standing in front of them now and I couldn't see their faces. I kept waving and looking in their direction, desperately hoping for one last glimpse.

The train chugged along the platform and I saw them again. At least, I saw the backs of their coats. Soldiers were herding them off the platform. Papa had his arm around Mama's shoulders. Their heads were bowed and they suddenly looked old and frail. And then more people surged behind them, and they were gone.

CHAPTER NINE

Look After
My Baby

I stood at the window as the train inched out of the station, staring numbly at the empty space where my parents had been.

When would I see them again? How would they manage without me?

I had promised to find them jobs. Would I really be able to do that?

I had to do it. I had no choice. Somehow, I would do it.

Something was happening. A young woman was running along the platform, weaving through the throng, her eyes wild and desperate.

As she drew level with our compartment, she caught my gaze and thrust a wicker hamper through the window at me. A picnic basket, I supposed, that her child had forgotten. I grabbed it and pulled it inside the compartment.

"Please," she called, running beside the train as it gathered speed, "please look after my baby. Take him to England. Please."

I stared at her. The train had almost left the platform. "His name is Ezra," she cried. "Ezra Neumann."

The train curved around a bend and the woman was out of sight. Numb with shock, I turned away from the window. The other children had sat down on the two wooden benches that faced each other across the compartment. Some of them were crying. The others gazed wide-eyed at the wicker basket clutched in my arms.

Wordlessly, two little children shuffled apart to make room for me. Wordlessly, I sat between them.

Every pair of eyes was fixed on the basket. Could there really be a baby in there?

Heart thumping, I fumbled with the leather strap and opened the lid.

Wrapped in a white blanket, sleeping like an angel, lay a tiny, black-haired baby. Tucked at the edge of the basket were two bottles of milk.

Panic rose inside me. I closed the lid and set the basket on the floor.

"I have to find an adult," I said.

I made my way along the empty corridor, peering through the glass panels in the compartment doors. Every compartment was crammed with children, but there wasn't a single adult. I seemed to be the oldest person in the carriage.

As I reached the final compartment, the lady with the clipboard came out of the door. Thank goodness!

"Excuse me," I said. "There's a baby in our compartment. What should I do with him?"

She looked stressed and flustered. "You'll have to look after him, I'm afraid. Older children need to take care of the younger ones."

"But I don't know how to look after a baby!"

She looked at me a little more kindly. "Does he have any food with him?"

"He has two bottles of milk."

"Excellent. And nappies?"

"I don't know."

"Well, you look like a sensible girl. I'm sure you'll cope. Use handkerchiefs if there aren't any clean nappies. Wash the soiled ones in the bathroom basin."

"But isn't there anybody else?"

"I'm sorry. There are only three adults on the train. We don't have time to look after the babies. I'm sure the other children in your compartment will help."

The other children looked up expectantly as I came back into the compartment. I picked up the wicker basket and settled it on my lap.

"We have to look after him ourselves," I said.

CHAPTER TEN

The Best Thing

To be honest, I'd never been very keen on babies. I couldn't understand why adults made such a fuss over them. They were usually quite ugly, they often smelled bad, and all they ever seemed to do was cry or sleep or dirty their nappies. Looking back, though, Ezra was the best thing that could have happened on that journey. He really helped distract us from our sadness and fears. And he was a very sweet baby. Lovely soft skin and amazing long eyelashes, and the cutest little rosebud mouth. Part of me wanted him to wake up, so that I could see his eyes, but the other part of me hoped he would sleep for a nice long time, because I really didn't have the faintest idea what to do once he was awake.

One of the smallest girls – she only looked about three – turned to me and said shyly, "Excuse me. I need the toilet."

A couple of the other children looked at me expectantly. With a start, I realised that, to them, I was an adult. They wanted me to take them to the toilet.

I stood up. "Does anybody else need the toilet?"

Four small children followed me out of the compartment. One little boy with a runny nose slipped his hand into mine.

"What's your name?" he asked.

"Anna," I said. "What's yours?"

"Ernst," he told me.

By the time we got back to the compartment, I knew all their names, and I asked the other children theirs too. That really helped to break the ice. They started to talk to each other. One girl, Ilse, who must only have been about seven, got out a handkerchief and dried the tears of a crying toddler. When he carried on crying, she picked him up and sat him on her lap and started to sing to him. I smiled at her and she smiled back.

One by one, the children fell asleep. Eventually, I felt myself falling asleep too, so I set the basket down on the floor at my feet.

I woke with a start. Ezra was crying.

I took one of the bottles out of the basket, picked him up and set him on my lap. I saw that underneath him, instead of a mattress, his mother had laid a pile of clean nappies. So I would be able to change him, as long as I could work out how to do it.

The other children slept on. I had never fed a baby before, but Ezra opened his little mouth as soon as I put the rubber teat against his lips, and he sucked the milk with complete concentration. As he drank, he looked at me intently. He had lovely brown eyes.

He drank almost half the bottle. I wondered how many more times he would need feeding.

The boy opposite me, Otto, was awake and looking at me. Earlier, he had said he was ten, which made him the second-oldest person in the compartment.

"Do you know how to change a nappy?" I whispered.

He shook his head. "But he must be wearing one at the moment, so when you take it off, you can figure out how it should be put on."

Of course! What a relief that there was somebody who could help. Between us, we worked out how to change a nappy. It was a nice feeling when Ezra was clean and dry and fed. He went straight back to sleep again. How lucky that he was such a peaceful baby.

I washed the nappy in the basin in the toilet, wrung it out and brought it back to the compartment to hang over the luggage rack to dry. By now, the sky was beginning to get light and some of the other children were starting to wake up and open their paper bags. As the food smells wafted around the compartment, I began to feel really hungry. I felt under my seat for my sandwiches. The sight of them, and the cake lovingly made by my mother, gave me a jolt of homesickness. I quickly pushed the feeling into the locked box in my head.

The journey went on and on. Most of us had finished our food by now, and some of the children were complaining of hunger. Otto had the clever idea of mixing Ezra's remaining milk with water, but even the watered-down milk wouldn't last much longer. I watched Ezra guzzle it with an anxious knot in my stomach.

"What will we do when it's all gone?"

"We'll just have to give him water," Otto said.

The little girl next to me, whose name was Eva, nudged me. "Look!"

She was pointing out of the window to a sign. "Three kilometres to the Dutch border."

Everybody looked tense and anxious.

"The Nazis don't let everybody across the border, you know," said Kurt, who was nine and thought he knew everything. "On the last transport, two boys were sent back on the next train, because their papers weren't in order."

Tears welled up in Ernst's eyes. I gave Kurt a fierce look. Then a terrible thought gripped my stomach.

What about Ezra? He had no papers.

My arms tightened around the basket. Nobody was going to take Ezra away from me.

CHAPTER ELEVEN

Open
the Basket

"Put the basket under your seat," said Walter, as though he could read my mind. "They might not see it there."

"Don't cry, Ezra," I whispered.

I closed the lid, pushed the basket under my seat and placed my feet in front of it.

The train drew into a station. The platform was swarming with SS men, all holding rifles with fixed bayonets glinting in the sunlight.

The second the train stopped, the soldiers pulled the doors open and jumped on board. In carriages further up the train, doors slammed, boots marched along the corridors and men barked orders.

Inside our compartment, everyone was silent. You could feel the tension in the air. Nobody moved. It felt as though nobody was even breathing.

The dreaded boots sounded in our corridor. A soldier appeared behind the glass. Eva jumped in fright as he flung the door open.

He pointed his rifle around the compartment. He had blond hair and a downy moustache. He looked very young.

"Take your cases down!"

Everyone got to their feet. Older children took down the younger ones' cases.

"Sit with your cases open on your knees."

We sat in petrified silence. Would he go through all our possessions? Would he steal our things? If he found something forbidden, would we get sent back?

The Nazis were capable of anything, we knew that by now.

And Ezra was definitely forbidden.

"Give me your money," the soldier ordered. "All of it."

I felt a surge of rage. How dare he demand the money our parents gave us?

But I said nothing. Nobody said anything. If we did, we might be sent back, or worse. So we all handed over the ten marks our parents had given us.

He pocketed the money without a word. Then his eye lighted on Franz's wristwatch.

"Hand over the watch! You know you were not allowed to bring anything of value."

Franz's fingers were trembling so much that he couldn't undo the leather strap. The soldier made an impatient gesture. Dorit, who sat between me and Franz, undid it for him. Franz, white-faced, handed the watch to the soldier. He pocketed it with the money.

Ernst began to cry. Ilse put her hand on his knee, but he pushed it away and wiped his sleeve across his eyes. I couldn't hear a single child anywhere on the train. All I could hear was guards giving orders, doors slamming, bangs and thumps.

The soldier's eyes roamed around the compartment and came to rest on Eva.

"Stand up," he ordered.

Eva slid off the seat.

"Give me your case."

She handed it over. Her hands were shaking.

He tipped all her beautifully pressed and folded clothes on to the floor. Eva gave a little cry, which she quickly stifled.

The soldier rifled through her clothes, shaking each item, presumably to check for hidden valuables. I felt a burning anger mixed with shame on Eva's behalf as her underwear was revealed to everyone in the compartment.

The man kicked the heap of clothes and ordered Eva to put everything back. She slid off her seat and knelt on the floor, stuffing her clothes back into the case. She glanced at him, white-faced, but he had lost interest in her. He was glaring at the basket under my seat.

"Whose is that?"

"Mine," I said, in a strange croaky voice that didn't sound like my own.

He jabbed his bayonet at me.

"Why do you have two cases? You are supposed to have one case only. Open the basket."

My heart was pounding so hard that I thought it might burst.

"Are you deaf?" he barked. "Open the basket."

I couldn't move.

He pointed his bayonet at the basket.

"No!" I yelled, leaping out of my seat. My case tumbled to the floor. "Don't hurt him!"

Ezra started to cry. I crouched down, pulled the basket out from under the seat and opened the lid.

"Where is the number?" asked the soldier.

I was silent. What could I say?

Ezra's cries grew louder. The soldier looked at him. He looked at me. Then, without a word, he turned his back and walked out of the compartment.

Nobody moved. Nobody spoke.

Had he gone to fetch a superior officer? Were we all doomed?

I picked Ezra up and held him tight. When I sat down, I felt Eva shaking beside me. Tears streamed down her cheeks. I put an arm around her shoulders and pulled her to me.

Otto bent down and picked up Ezra's almost-empty bottle. He handed it to me and I popped the teat in the baby's open mouth. He stopped crying and sucked noisily.

Doors clanged. SS men swarmed out on to the platform. The train started to move. Did that mean we were safe?

The train slowed to a stop. I felt sick.

It started to move again.

Then it stopped. There was the sound of clunking metal. I held my breath. Slowly, agonisingly slowly, the train began to move again. And then I saw a sign. We were at the Dutch border.

Please don't stop now, I prayed. *Please cross the border. Please take us out of Germany.*

CHAPTER TWELVE

Holland!

The train jolted forwards. Another sign appeared ahead of us.

Holland! We were in Holland!

From further up the train, we heard cheering and whooping. We glanced at each other. Could we really be safe?

The train slowed again. We were coming into a station. The platform was full of smiling, waving women. We stared at each other in disbelief. Were they really smiling and waving at us?

The train stopped. Doors opened. Two women came into our compartment. One looked about Mama's age and the other was much older, with a smiling, wrinkled face. They carried big baskets, and from them they handed round cheese sandwiches, shiny red apples and chocolate bars, smiling at us and speaking kind words we couldn't understand. The little children looked amazed, and some of them glanced at me to see if it was all right to take the food. I nodded and smiled at them.

The older lady cooed over Ezra. Even though I didn't understand Dutch, I could tell she was saying what a lovely baby he was. I smiled with pride. Then I held up the empty bottle. "Do you have any milk, please?" I asked, hoping she would understand, even if she didn't speak German.

She did understand. Smiling, she produced a large bottle of milk from her basket. She took Ezra's bottle, filled it to the brim and held out her arms for him. I hesitated for a second, and then handed him over. She tucked him expertly into the crook of her arm and popped the teat into his mouth.

The younger lady handed round paper cups and filled them with lemonade. It was the most delicious lemonade I had ever tasted. With the older lady looking after Ezra, I took a bite of my sandwich. The bread was thickly spread with butter and was the best food I had ever tasted.

The older lady handed Ezra back to me with a smile. Both ladies gave out the last of the food from their baskets, hugged each of us in turn and kissed the tops of our heads. They waved a final goodbye as they left the compartment. All the other women were getting off the train too. They stood on the platform, waving to us through the windows as the train began to move.

A picture came into my head of my own family, my parents' faces on the platform, their brave, forced smiles. I pushed the image away and looked around the compartment.

All the tension had gone. The children were dozing, their heads on each other's shoulders. I glanced at Eva, who was leaning against the window. She was dozing too.

Ezra slept soundly in my arms. I leaned down and pulled the basket out from under the seat. Very gently, I placed him in the basket, tucking the blanket around him. He continued to sleep.

As I leaned back in my seat, I felt as though a great weight that I didn't even know I'd been carrying had been lifted from my shoulders. To my surprise, I found myself crying. Strangely, it was a relief to cry. It actually felt comforting. The tension in my body melted away and I was left with an exhaustion so heavy that I couldn't keep my eyes open any longer.

CHAPTER THIRTEEN

Where Are His Papers?

I woke with a jerk. Everything was dark. There were sounds of clanking metal and raised voices. The train wasn't moving. Eva's head lay heavy on my shoulder. Compartment doors were opening. There was a jumble of voices, but I couldn't make out any words.

The others were waking up too, moving and stretching, opening their eyes. Eva lifted her head from my shoulder. I looked down and saw that Ezra was still sleeping.

"Where are we?" I asked Otto.

The compartment door opened. My stomach lurched as a man in uniform appeared from the shadows. But it wasn't Nazi uniform. And he was smiling.

"Gather all your belongings," he said, "and be ready to leave the train when you are told to do so."

He spoke in German, but with a foreign accent. I wanted to ask him where we were but, even though he looked friendly, I couldn't bring myself to trust him. I waited until he'd left the compartment, and then I asked Otto again.

"I think we're at the coast," he said.

I had always wanted to see the sea. But this boat journey would take me even further away from my parents.

Luckily, there was no time to think. We were told to leave the train, and Otto and I were busy buttoning up the little ones' coats and checking under the seats in case anything had been left. I took the rinsed-out nappies from where I had hung them to dry on the luggage rack. They were still damp. I folded them and put them in my coat pocket. Hopefully there would be somewhere warm on the boat to dry them.

Otto carried my suitcase so I could carry Ezra's basket. The lighted platform was full of kind, smiling faces. It felt as though we really would be safe now.

We stood in line on the platform for a long time, slowly shuffling towards a table where two smiling Jewish Agency ladies sat with lists in front of them. They were checking each child's label and the matching label on their suitcase.

Otto was in front of me. When his name had been ticked off the list, the lady indicated for him to move forward and join the next line. He shot an anxious glance at Ezra as he walked off.

The ladies smiled at me. They checked my labels and ticked my name off the list. Then the younger one said, in German, "And what do you have in the basket?"

I panicked. "Nothing."

"Shall we have a look?" asked the younger lady

kindly. She stood up and reached for the basket. I clutched it more tightly. She opened the lid.

"Oh! The dearest little baby!"

The other lady peered into the basket. She smiled and cooed at Ezra.

"Your brother or sister?" asked the young lady.

I shook my head, and then immediately cursed myself. Why was I so stupid? If I'd said he was my brother, perhaps they would have let me take him through.

But it was too late now.

"He's called Ezra," I said. "Ezra Neumann."

"Can you show me his papers?" the lady asked.

I stared at her dumbly.

"Do you have his papers?"

I shook my head.

"Where are his papers then? Who has them?"

"I... I don't know."

She frowned. "What did you say his name was?"

"Ezra Neumann."

She ran her finger down the list of names. For a split second, I had a brief, crazy surge of hope, like a flash of sunlight through the clouds. Maybe his name *was* on the list. Maybe his mother had registered him for the transport but had forgotten to pack his papers in the basket.

The lady shook her head. "His name isn't here. How is it that you're looking after him?"

I would have to tell the truth. Surely they wouldn't send him back?

"His mother gave him to me. She handed him

through the train window. I promised I'd look after him."

She turned and spoke to the other lady in Dutch. They called another lady over. She looked at Ezra and they all held an intense conversation. Then the one who spoke German turned to me and said, very kindly, "Because the baby was not expected, no arrangements have been made for him. Therefore, we think the best thing to do would be to put him in an orphanage here in Holland and—"

"No!" I shouted. "You can't put him in an orphanage! His mother gave him to me to look after. I won't leave him!"

I grabbed Ezra from his basket and clutched him to me. The ladies looked startled. I felt startled. Had I really screamed like that? But I couldn't stop now.

"If the English people will take hundreds of children into their homes, surely they will take one little baby! I promised his mother I would take him to England. You can't take him away from me."

The ladies stared at me. I stared back, the baby in my arms. I felt fierce and strong, grown up all of a sudden.

The older lady said something to me in Dutch, clearly trying to calm me down.

They had a murmured conversation. Then the young woman touched my arm.

"We will see what can be done. Come over here, while we register the other children. Don't worry. We will sort something out."

She took me by the arm and led me towards a

bench beside the ticket office. Cold fear crept over me. What if they made me stay in Holland too? What if they put both of us in an orphanage?

I pulled away from her and walked back to the table.

"I'm going to England," I said, "and so is Ezra. I'm going to wait here."

It took a long time. An endless queue of exhausted children, some crying, some almost asleep on their feet, filed slowly past the table, as the list filled up with ticks. Ezra woke and started to cry. I gave him the rest of the milk and went to the waiting room to change his nappy. I washed the wet nappy in the sink, wrung it out and tied it around the handle of my suitcase to dry. When I walked back to the table, the kind German-speaking lady looked up and smiled at me.

"We will send a telegraph to the British authorities," she said. "We will make arrangements. Do not worry. You can take the baby to England."

CHAPTER FOURTEEN

White Cake and
Bitter Coffee

Even in that awful situation, it was exciting to be on a boat. Most of us had never seen the sea, and lots of the children went crazy, running up and down the staircases, above and below deck, exploring every corner of the ship. I secretly wished I could too, but I had to look after Ezra. The sailors were so kind and helpful. They warmed up his milk, gave us supper and gave up their own bunks so we could sleep. Ezra and I had a little cabin to ourselves. I was so exhausted and it was so lovely to lie down that I fell asleep instantly.

When I first woke up, I had no idea where I was. Then I saw my parents' hunched, defeated backs on the station platform, and my insides felt hollow again.

I forced the image into the box and locked it away. Ezra was still sleeping peacefully.

I lifted the blind that covered the porthole. Dazzling light flooded into the cabin. Outside, diamonds of light danced on a sparkling sheet of water that stretched on and on to a fiery pink and gold glow on the horizon. The sun was beginning to rise over the English Channel.

It was the most beautiful thing I had ever seen. A sudden feeling of joy surged through me.

"We're free!" I whispered to Ezra. "We're in England and we're free!"

Then I felt dreadful. My parents weren't free.

Soon, I told myself. Soon they would be free, too.

Once I was dressed and had changed Ezra's nappy, I found my way to the lounge. The ship was in dock, but the sailors were giving us breakfast before we left. When a steward saw me with the baby, he gave me a big smile and showed me to a seat at a table. He made the other children move along to make room for me. I showed him Ezra's empty bottle and said the sentence I had practised as I was getting dressed. "Please may I have more milk?"

"Oh, you speak English!" He sounded surprised.

"A little," I said, but inside I swelled with pride.

He took the bottle. "Have some breakfast." He indicated a plate on the table, heaped with thin slices of some sort of plain cake spread with butter. Then he went off to fill the bottle.

"What is it?" I asked the other children.

"I don't know," said a girl. "It's very strange."

"It's horrible," said a little boy, screwing up his face.

"It's good," said an older boy, with his mouth full, as he reached for another slice.

"But why would they spread cake with butter?"

He shrugged. "Try it."

He pushed the plate across the table. I took a slice

and sniffed it. The butter didn't smell like butter. Gingerly, I took a little bite. The white cake was soft and spongy and bland. Whatever was spread on it had the texture of butter but tasted different. It was all quite strange, but it wasn't really horrible. Besides, I was hungry.

"Were you seasick?" asked a girl.

"No," I said. "I was asleep."

"Lucky you," she said. "I was sick all night."

The nice steward appeared, carrying Ezra's bottle filled with warm milk. He handed me a cup of steaming coffee.

"Thank you," I said in English, and he smiled at me.

I took a sip and spluttered. It wasn't coffee. It had a horrible bitter taste. The other children laughed. Luckily, the steward had left. I wouldn't have liked him to think I was being rude.

"What is it?" I asked. "I thought it was coffee."

"It's tea," said an older girl opposite me. "The steward said English people drink tea with milk in it."

"It's disgusting," I said. But I made myself drink half of it, so as not to seem ungrateful.

When the steward returned to clear our plates, I decided to try out my English again.

"What is the name of this cake?"

He laughed. I felt mortified. What had I said wrong?

"That's not cake," he said. "It's bread and butter."

I stared at him. Was he joking? At home, we ate

rye bread, dark and dense, with a strong, rich flavour. This white spongy stuff in thin slices wasn't like bread at all. I hoped everything in England wasn't going to feel so alien.

After breakfast was cleared away, the lounge became a sort of office. Several smartly dressed ladies came on to the boat and sat at a table. We had to wait in line again while they checked our papers and gave us all another label. This time, the labels had our names on.

While I was waiting, I used my dictionary to help me work out what to say to the ladies about Ezra. I didn't want to be unprepared, like I had been in Holland. So when it came to my turn, and the elegant woman in the fur coat looked at Ezra and said, "And who is this?" I was able to reply, "His name is Ezra Neumann. He has no papers. The women in Holland said they would speak to you on the telephone."

The woman in the fur coat smiled at me. "You speak English very well. I did speak to Frau Weissmuller in Holland. My colleague, Mrs Simons, is going to look after the baby until we can find him a permanent home. She will be there to meet him in London. Can you look after him until we get there?"

Perhaps she was making a special effort to speak clearly, but I was really proud that although I couldn't understand every word, I could catch her general meaning.

"Yes, I can," I told her.

She smiled again. "That would be very helpful."

But I wasn't doing it to be helpful. I just wanted to

keep Ezra for as long as possible.

An official man stamped our papers and another man in uniform stamped the label. The sight of them in their uniforms made my stomach tense up, but these men were very different from German officials. They didn't shout, and sometimes they even smiled at us. And when the man who stamped the labels accidentally stepped on a boy's foot, he apologised to the boy! We all gaped at him.

I was impatient to get off the boat and see England. But when we walked down the gangplank on to the quayside, we had to stand in line again while the British customs officers searched our luggage.

By the time we got on the train, it was early afternoon. I was excited to see the English countryside, and to catch my first glimpse of London. I wondered if we would be able to see Buckingham Palace, the Houses of Parliament or Tower Bridge, all the places I knew from my books.

But as soon as I sat down on the comfortable upholstered seats (upholstered seats! Were we in First Class?) and settled Ezra's basket on the floor, a wave of exhaustion swept over me. The rhythm of the train and the sound of the engine sent me straight to sleep.

CHAPTER FIFTEEN

Welcome to England

I woke up as we drew in to Liverpool Street Station, a vast glass-roofed space swirling with steam. Ezra was still sleeping. I bent to pick up his basket, but a lady who spoke German came into our compartment and said, "Thank you for looking after the baby. I'll take him now."

"But what's going to happen to him?"

"Mrs Simons will meet us here and take him home. He'll be very well looked after, don't you worry."

"But how will his mother know where to find him?"

"We'll keep all his details at Bloomsbury House," she said.

Before I could ask any more, a whistle blew and we were ushered out of the train into a huge crowd of people waiting on the platform. Immediately, people began shouting and waving. Eva, who was going to stay with her auntie, cried, "Tante Rosi, Tante Rosi!" and a small, dark-haired woman turned around and beamed, throwing her arms wide open as Eva pushed through the crowd. She swept Eva into an enormous hug. I looked at them and felt sick with loneliness and longing.

The ladies in charge were desperately trying to keep order. One of them close to me blew a whistle that nearly deafened me. Everybody on the platform was startled into silence. In a loud voice, she gave what were clearly instructions, though I couldn't understand most of the words. Then she gestured for everybody to follow her.

She led us to a vast, gloomy underground room below the station. Another lady handed each of us a paper bag. Inside were sandwiches, made with that funny white bread again, and also an apple and an orange, which was nice. We had to sit in rows in one part of the room while our new foster parents sat in another part, behind a rope barrier. The list was in alphabetical order so, with the surname Schlesinger, I guessed I'd be waiting for hours.

I sat there, cradling my orange. I couldn't see anybody from my compartment on the German train, and it felt so strange not to be looking after Ezra any more. I looked all around the hall but I couldn't see him anywhere. The mysterious Mrs Simons must have already taken him home with her. I hadn't even said goodbye. Tears prickled my eyelids, but I bit my cheeks and blinked them back.

I couldn't just sit there, getting more and more anxious about meeting my foster parents. I had to distract myself somehow. I could read *Heidi*, but I was too nervous to concentrate on a book.

Then I remembered. I hadn't written to my parents. I'd promised them I'd write on the train.

I felt a terrible wave of guilt. I quickly opened my case and got out my writing things.

Writing to Mama and Papa was wonderfully comforting. It almost felt like talking to them. I told them all about Ezra and the lovely Dutch ladies and the kind sailors. I didn't put in any of the bad stuff.

When I eventually finished and looked up from the paper, I was surprised to see hardly any children left in the huge room. One of the organisers called out, "Renate Woolf?"

Woolf? They'd reached W? But where was my family? Had they changed their minds? Had they forgotten me? Had I not heard when they'd called my name, because I'd been so absorbed in my letter? But wouldn't somebody have come and found me?

Perhaps I should walk over to the curtained-off part of the room where the smart ladies sat, and ask them why I hadn't been called. But they might be annoyed if I did that. And what if they told me the family didn't want me after all? If that was going to be the news, I didn't want to hear it.

I sat there, gripping the edges of the hard wooden bench, hovering half off the seat in an agony of indecision.

"Anna Schlesinger?"

I looked up. One of the ladies smiled and beckoned me towards the curtained-off area.

"Would you like me to put a stamp on this and post it for you?" she said, looking at the envelope clutched in my hand.

"Yes, please," I said gratefully. "Thank you very much."

My stomach churned and my hands were damp with sweat as I walked up to the other end of the hall and behind the big tarpaulins.

Another lady looked at me across a table covered with papers.

"Anna Schlesinger?"

"Yes." My voice was a croak.

"Anna, this is Mrs Dean, your foster mother."

She gestured to a pretty, plump woman with wavy dark hair and a warm smile, who hurried over and gave me a big hug. Relief flooded over me. A kind foster mother!

Mrs Dean picked up my case and started talking to me in very fast English. I couldn't understand a word she said. The lady at the table said something to her. I think she must have been telling her I didn't speak much English, because when Mrs Dean turned back to me, she spoke more slowly.

"Welcome to England, Anna. It's so lovely to meet you."

CHAPTER SIXTEEN

Kent

After the cold and gloom of the underground room, it was dizzying to walk out on to the hot and noisy London street. Immediately, a big red bus drew up in front of us: a double-decker bus, just like I had seen in pictures!

Mrs Dean led me on to the bus and we sat right at the front, on the top deck. It was wonderful to look down on the London streets, with their grand grey buildings and the people walking briskly along the pavements. She asked me about the journey and I couldn't remember how to say "long", so I just said, "It was good, thank you." Then I said, "Do you live in London?"

Mrs Dean threw back her head and laughed.

"Oh, bless you, no!" She said something I couldn't understand, and she must have noticed my blank expression, because she slowed her voice down and said, "We live in the countryside. Do you understand?"

I nodded. I was a bit disappointed that I wasn't going to stay in London, but Mama always said the English countryside was very beautiful.

"We have to get another train," Mrs Dean said. "We live in Kent. In a village called Ashcombe."

I wondered whom she meant by "we". Would it be rude to ask whether she had children?

My curiosity got the better of me.

"Do you have children?" I asked.

She smiled at me. "You speak English very well. Yes, we have two children. Frank is seven and Molly's twelve. That's why we chose you. We thought it would be nice for Molly to have a friend the same age."

I was really pleased that I could understand that. At least, I hoped I'd understood it. I tried to picture Molly and Frank. I imagined them as smaller versions of Mrs Dean, with dark wavy hair and smiling, rosy faces.

We got off the bus at another busy station, and within a few minutes we were on a train again.

"We thought it would be nice," said Mrs Dean, as she unwrapped a paper parcel of sandwiches, "if you called me Aunty Rose. And my husband you can call Uncle Bert."

I nodded and smiled. "Thank you," I said, taking one of the sandwiches she offered. I didn't like to tell her we'd been given sandwiches at the station. Besides, I didn't know how long it would be until my next meal.

The upholstered seats were so comfortable that I could easily have gone to sleep, but I wanted to see the English countryside this time.

First, the train crossed a wide grey river. I pointed

at it.

"River Thames?"

Mrs Dean – Aunty Rose – gave a big smile. "Well done!"

On the other side of the river, we passed a lot of dull grey buildings and rows of little houses. Then the houses stopped and the train was steaming through the countryside. And it was so beautiful.

Bright-green fields were sprinkled with masses of wild flowers, pink and yellow and white. White blossoms foamed in the dense green hedgerows. We passed lovely stone churches, and little houses where the roofs seemed to be made of straw. Were they really made of straw? I wanted to ask Aunty Rose, but I didn't know the words. I rifled through my dictionary, but by the time I had found the word for "straw", we had passed the houses.

By the time we finally got out at a tiny station, the light was starting to fade and there was nobody else around.

"We have to get another bus now," said Mrs Dean, carrying my case to a painted bus stop sign with a wooden bench beside it. So the journey still wasn't over! She said something that was probably an explanation of where we were going, but I couldn't understand a word.

Opposite the station, the hands on the church clock stood at ten to nine. The quiet evening air was so fresh and sweet after the grimy coal-dust smell of the trains. The only sounds were the buzzing of insects and an endless choir of birds, twittering and chattering, cawing and cooing, chirruping and singing, in the hedges and trees and sky. One pair of birds soared higher and higher above me, singing all the way.

Aunty Rose saw me looking at them and smiled. "Larks," she said, pointing upwards. Then came a rumbling sound along the road. "Oh, good," she said. "The bus."

In the fading light, the bus trundled past more lovely fields and woods, along narrow lanes lined with wild flowers, where the high canopies of the trees on either side joined together in places to form an arch.

It was almost dark when we got off the bus. Mrs Dean took a torch out of her bag and switched it on.

A silver crescent moon hung high in the sky. The same moon, I thought. The same moon that's shining above my parents.

I sent a silent message to the moon. *Please keep my parents safe.*

I could hear occasional sounds of sheep and cows in the fields around us. As we walked along the lane, the smell of manure grew stronger and stronger. I wrinkled my nose, and then hoped Mrs Dean hadn't seen me do it.

To the right of the lane I saw shadowy outlines of what must be farm buildings. There was a big wooden barn and some other low-roofed buildings that might be stables.

Aunty Rose opened a wide wooden gate that led off the lane into a farmyard.

"Here we are," she said. "Welcome to Ashcombe, Anna."

I stared at her in surprise. She hadn't said they lived on a farm. Or maybe she had, but I hadn't understood.

We walked through the farmyard. The smell of manure was even stronger here. Grunting noises came from somewhere nearby. Pigs? I wasn't sure I wanted to live so close to pigs. I'd always found them a bit scary.

"Frank should be in bed, of course," said Aunty Rose, "but I expect he's stayed up to see you. And Molly will be dying to meet you."

Her torch beam lit up a little white gate in a hedge at the far side of the yard. She opened the gate and we walked up a short path and then around the edge of a house to a low door at the back. It opened into a narrow room with a long wooden work surface and a big sink under the window. In the light of the torch beam, I saw bowls and jugs, and shelves stacked with jars.

Mrs Dean opened another door into a cosy kitchen, lit only by an oil lamp in the middle of the table. Around the table sat a man and two children, playing cards.

"Hello, everybody," said Mrs Dean. "This is Anna."

The man put down his cards and came forward. He was short like his wife, but slim and wiry, with a kind, warm smile.

"Welcome, Anna," he said, taking both my hands

in his. "We're so pleased to see you."

"And this is Frank," said Aunty Rose, bending down and giving the boy a kiss. He had messy brown hair and a round freckled face. He gave me a shy smile.

"Well, say hello to Anna," said Uncle Bert. "You've been pestering me all day, asking when she'd be here."

Frank squirmed. "Hello, Anna," he said.

I smiled at him to show I was friendly. "Hello, Frank."

Frank beamed. "She speaks English! You said she wouldn't, but she does!"

"A little," I said, and Frank beamed again.

"Anna speaks English very well," said Aunty Rose. "Just remember to speak clearly and slowly, so she can understand you."

"And this is Molly," said Uncle Bert.

I had wanted to look properly at Molly before, but for politeness' sake I had focused on greeting Uncle Bert and Frank. Now I saw she had a friendly, freckled face like Frank. She smiled and stood up. She was wearing trousers! I looked at them enviously. I wondered how it felt to wear trousers.

"Hello, Anna," said Molly, and she walked around the table and gave me a hug. Her parents smiled proudly.

Uncle Bert said something to Aunty Rose that I couldn't understand. She replied and then turned to me. "Would you like some food, Anna, or would you like to go to bed?"

I suddenly realised how exhausted I was.

"I would like to go to bed, please."

"I'll show you our room," said Molly.

From the cupboard by the stove she took a candle in a tin saucer. She lit it and beckoned me to follow her.

A candle?

I looked around. There were no lights on the walls or ceiling.

Did English houses not have electricity? Nobody had told me that.

We walked up a narrow staircase and into a little bedroom with two beds and a pine chest of drawers between them. There was a rug on the floorboards and a shelf with a few books.

"That's your bed," said Molly, pointing to the one on the left. Then she opened the middle drawer of the chest, which was empty. "And that's for your things."

"Thank you," I said.

"Is there anything else you need?"

"Where is the bathroom, please?" I asked.

She gave me a funny look. "We don't have a bathroom. There's a lav in the garden."

I looked at her, puzzled. Had I asked the question wrong?

"I'll show you," she said.

She led me downstairs again and said something to Aunty Rose, who looked mortified. "Oh, Anna, I'm so sorry. I should have shown you."

She took her torch off the hook by the back door

and led me down a path through the back garden. At the bottom of the garden was a small square shed.

"There you are," she said, handing me the torch. She patted me on the shoulder and headed back up the path.

Gingerly, I lifted the latch and opened the door. Inside the shed was a wooden bench with a round hole in the centre of it. Underneath this hole was a metal bucket.

I stared at it in horror. This was a toilet? This was how people lived in England? No electricity and no bathrooms?

A desperate, miserable longing came over me as I pictured our beautiful apartment and all our lovely things.

And then I thought of how the Nazis had come in the middle of the night and smashed it all to pieces.

I have no home any more, I thought, as I trudged back up the garden path.

And I got into my little bed and cried myself to sleep.

CHAPTER SEVENTEEN

A Plan

Sunlight filtered through the thin curtains. Birds chattered shrilly outside the window.

Molly's bed was empty, the sheets and blankets rumpled. The heavy woollen blankets on my bed felt so strange after my soft feather quilt at home.

I locked away the thoughts of home. What time was it? Had I slept late?

I got out of bed and opened the curtains.

A green patchwork of fields stretched into the distance, the meadows dotted with bright-yellow flowers that shone in the sunlight. Sheep and lambs grazed in one field and brown cows in another. Long wisps of white cloud, like soft brushstrokes in a painted landscape, floated through the blue sky.

Gazing at the landscape, I felt a sudden sensation of peace and permanence. This place seemed like a fairytale kingdom, protected from the outside world. A place where nothing bad could ever happen.

I had to bring my parents here. I had to find a way.

And then I noticed something else.

In the distance, away to my right on a slight rise in the land beyond a cluster of tall trees, stood an enormous stone house. A house so huge that you couldn't really call it a house. It was more like a palace.

Who lived there? It must be somebody incredibly rich.

My eyes opened wide and I drew in my breath.

Rich people needed servants. And now I had a plan.

CHAPTER EIGHTEEN

Foamy White Flowers
and Lumpy White Gloop

By the time Molly and I climbed over the locked gate into Lord Hurstwood's kitchen garden, exactly two weeks later, I knew that the foamy white flowers in the hedgerow were elderflowers. Not only did I know what they were; I knew how to make elderflower cordial by stirring the flower heads in a big pan with lemons, sugar and boiling water and then straining them through a muslin cloth.

I knew a lot of other things, too, that I hadn't known two weeks ago. I knew that wearing trousers instead of dresses made me feel as though I could do anything and go anywhere. Wearing trousers made me want to swagger down the road with my hands in my pockets and have an adventure, instead of staying at home being a good girl and doing what I was told. No wonder men ruled the world.

I also knew that, instead of flushing the toilet, I had to tip a mixture of soil and ash into the bucket, and that I had to wash my hands in freezing water from the pump in the room that I now knew was called the scullery. I knew that bath time happened once a week, and involved a tin bath in front of the kitchen stove, filled with hot water from the big kettle and screened by the towel rail. And I knew I was lucky that, as the guest, I got to use the water first.

I knew now that sheep were generally harmless, and that you could push your hand so far down into their woolly coats that it disappeared up to the wrist before you touched their skin. I knew to keep out of the way of the cows with their terrifying horns when they were herded from the field into the cowshed twice a day for milking. I knew to keep out of the way of Jim the cow man too, but that Matthew the pig man was friendly and occasionally even gave us toffees.

I knew that Bess and Bonnie, the two farm horses, were gentle and quiet, and liked having their noses stroked. I knew that piglets were very sweet-looking but squealed like banshees if you picked them up. I knew, because Molly kept telling me so, that the geese wouldn't actually hurt me, but I still couldn't help running when they lowered their great necks and waddled towards me, flapping their wings and hissing through their sharp serrated beaks.

I knew that Molly loved all the animals, especially the chickens she kept in the garden. I knew better than to let her know I found the hens repulsive, with their mess and their flapping and those dangling bits of red skin hanging from their faces. I pretended I found them beautiful, in the same way I pretended to like the disgusting lumpy white gloop called porridge that the Deans ate for breakfast. Luckily,

I also knew that Aunty Rose was a very good cook, and dinner and tea were a lot better than breakfast.

I knew that Uncle Bert was the carpenter on the Ashcombe estate, and that when he wasn't fixing things on the estate he was either fixing things in the house, working in the garden or making wooden toys for Frank. I knew that Aunty Rose, as well as cooking for the family and doing all the housework, made jam and bread and cakes to sell at the WI market in the nearest town every Saturday. I knew that Uncle Bert and Aunty Rose were hard-working and kind and fun, and that I was very lucky to be living with them.

I knew that Frank loved vehicles and gardening, and spent most of his free time either playing with the toy cars and trucks and planes Uncle Bert made for him, or tending his patch of garden. I knew that Molly loved animal stories and adventure novels, and that she got real satisfaction from helping me with my English. On my very first day, after I had asked, "What is this called, please?" about a hundred times, she suddenly said, "Wait a minute." Then she fetched some empty paper bags from a drawer, cut them into strips and took me around the house as she labelled every object and piece of furniture and made sure I could pronounce the names correctly.

I knew I wouldn't be starting school until September, because there were only two weeks left of the summer term and Aunty Rose felt it would be better for me to start at the beginning of the school year, once my English had improved. I was grateful for this, and I enjoyed the days helping her in the house and garden. She gave me some of Frank and Molly's old books to help with my English too. I couldn't wait to master the language so I could borrow Molly's adventure stories.

I knew that Molly's black-and-white cat, Clover, for some reason known only to herself, had decided to adopt me as her pet. Everybody else knew this too, since, on my very first morning, Clover jumped on to my lap and sat there, purring loudly, while the rest of the family looked on in amazement.

"Well, she loves you, Anna," said Aunty Rose. "She's never sat on anybody's lap before."

Now, as soon as I sat down in the kitchen or sat in bed to read or write letters, Clover would appear as if by magic and settle on my lap. I was sure she could sense that I was missing my family. Although Molly didn't say anything, I knew she wasn't too pleased that her cat had defected to me. But there wasn't much I could do about it. Cats make their own decisions.

I knew that if I felt a sudden wave of homesickness during the day, then I could generally lock it away and distract myself by helping in the house or garden. But I also knew, having already received two long and loving letters from my parents, that there was no way to control the homesickness that flooded over me when I read their letters. The only thing to do then was to find a quiet place to cry until the tears stopped.

I knew, too, that I couldn't control my nightmares,

where storm troopers and SS men dragged my parents away from me, while I tried to attack the soldiers but found I couldn't move, and I tried to scream for help but my voice made no sound.

Some nights I woke in a cold sweat, shivering. Some nights I woke screaming. Molly was an amazingly heavy sleeper and my screams rarely woke her, but Aunty Rose always came in. She would sit on the end of my bed, murmuring soothing sounds and stroking my hair until eventually I went back to sleep.

She never asked what the nightmares were about, and she never mentioned it in the morning. I was grateful for that. I didn't want to talk about it.

I knew, too, that most people thought England would soon be at war with Germany. And so, more than anything else, I knew I had to get my parents to England. Every day I looked up words in my dictionary and practised the English I would need to put my plan into action.

Which was why, right now, Molly and I were creeping past Lord Hurstwood's raspberry canes and heading towards the huge front door of Ashcombe House itself.

CHAPTER NINETEEN

Ashcombe House

Luckily, the elderly gardener had his back to us. We managed to sneak all the way up the kitchen garden to a path that ran around the edge of the house. I started to head to the right, but Molly grabbed my sleeve.

"That's the stable block," she whispered. "There's bound to be a boy mucking out."

So we crept around the other side, between flowerbeds where glorious pink and white roses, their blooms as big as teacups, scented the air. I heard Mama's voice in my head, saying, "English gardens are the finest in the world," and I had to remind myself to breathe as I followed Molly up the front steps.

When I'd first had my idea, I'd planned to keep it secret. I was afraid that if I told anyone, they would try to stop me. But when Molly grew impatient with my carefully rehearsed questions and asked why I was so interested in Lord and Lady Hurstwood, I decided it was time to tell her.

I couldn't understand half her response, because Molly spoke so fast when she was excited, but I understood that she thought it was a good plan and she wanted to be involved.

To Molly, this was all an adventure. She had no idea how important it was to get my parents out of Germany. That wasn't her fault. Even if I'd wanted to open the locked box inside my head, which I didn't, I couldn't have explained, in my limited English, how bad the situation was.

But I was glad to have her with me. Even though I had studied and practised what I would say, I wasn't sure I'd understand what anybody said to me in reply. And I was scared too. Scared of knocking on the door of this vast, grand house. Scared that if they refused to listen to me, then I would have lost the one hope I had of helping my parents.

Ever since the idea had come into my head on my first morning at Ashcombe, it had been my all-consuming dream. I couldn't wait for the day when I could write to tell Mama and Papa I had found jobs for them in England.

And I was terrified of messing it up.

Molly lifted the gleaming brass knocker and rapped on the enormous oak door. My stomach writhed with nerves.

The door was opened by a tall, elegant man in an immaculate black suit. He looked completely calm and in control, exactly as I had imagined an English lord. I was slightly disappointed that he wasn't wearing an ermine cloak and a crown, like all the lords had worn for King George's coronation. But the cloak and crown were just for special occasions, I supposed.

Trying to suppress my nerves, I forced a polite smile.

"Good morning, Lord Hurstwood."

The man's eyes widened slightly. Molly elbowed me in the ribs. What had I done wrong?

She gave the man an ingratiating smile and said, "Good morning, sir. We are here to speak with Lord Hurstwood, please."

So this man wasn't Lord Hurstwood. Well, how could I have known that? But it explained why he was just wearing a plain suit. I wondered who he was. I hoped he wasn't offended that I'd mistaken him for Lord Hurstwood.

"Lord Hurstwood is expecting us," Molly continued. "We're here on urgent business."

The man raised his eyebrows very slightly, in an amused, superior sort of way.

"I'm afraid Lord Hurstwood is not at home," he said.

"Could we speak to Lady Hurstwood then?" said Molly. "It's very urgent."

The man raised his eyebrows slightly higher.

"And is Lady Hurstwood expecting you too?"

"Yes," said Molly, giving him a look that dared him to challenge her.

"I'm afraid Lady Hurstwood is otherwise engaged."

I wasn't sure what "otherwise engaged" meant, but his tone wasn't very welcoming.

"That's all right," said Molly. "We can wait."

"I'm afraid Lady Hurstwood will be engaged for some time," said the man.

"What's that, Robins?" said a woman's voice. "Engaged with what?"

A lady was standing in the doorway at the back of the hall. She had wavy brown hair and an interested, friendly face, the kind of face that looked as if it smiled a lot.

She looked enquiringly at the man. He dipped his head slightly and spoke to her. She walked towards us. Was this Lady Hurstwood? She wore a simple blue dress and no jewellery and didn't seem grand at all. I felt my hopes rising. Might this kind-looking lady give a job to my parents?

She smiled at Molly.

"You're Mr Dean's daughter, aren't you? Molly, isn't it?"

"Yes, madam," she said.

The lady smiled at me. "I must apologise," she said. (Apologise? To me?) "I don't think we've met."

"My name is Anna," I said. "Anna Schlesinger."

"Anna's a German refugee, Lady Hurstwood," said Molly. "She came to England on the Kindertransport and she's staying with us. And we came to see you because—" She stopped and turned to me. "You tell it, Anna."

My stomach churned. I couldn't meet Lady Hurstwood's eyes.

"My... My parents need jobs in England. Germany is very dangerous for Jews at the moment. They are trying to leave but they need jobs and a visa. I... I wondered if you…"

I glanced at Lady Hurstwood. Her face was full of concern and sympathy. To my horror, I felt my throat tightening and my eyes filling up with tears. I bit my cheeks.

Lady Hurstwood took both my hands in hers.

"Oh, my dear," she said. "I'm so sorry."

That was it. I started to sob. Lady Hurstwood kept hold of my hands and led me into another room, saying something to the man as she did so. She sat me down on a sofa and handed me a handkerchief.

After a while, when my sobs had turned into hiccupy shudders, Lady Hurstwood patted me on the knee and said, "Have some tea, my dear."

A tea tray had magically appeared on the low table in front of the sofa. There was a silver teapot and three pretty china cups and saucers. There was also a plate of delicious-looking biscuits, but I had no appetite.

"Sugar?" she asked, picking up a pair of little silver tongs.

"Yes, please." I had discovered that I could tolerate English tea if it had sugar in it.

Molly was sitting on the sofa opposite. I didn't dare look at her. I had completely messed up my carefully practised plans.

Lady Hurstwood talked while she poured the tea and handed round the biscuits. I didn't understand everything, but Molly repeated it to me more slowly afterwards.

"My husband and I had some wonderful walking

holidays in Germany when we were first married. Such a beautiful country. Such lovely people. It's just terrible, what's happening at the moment. It's as though that dreadful man has bewitched everybody. The whole country seems to have gone mad."

A door banged somewhere nearby and a man's voice said, "Down, Audrey! Flora, come here, you blasted nuisance!"

A brown-and-white spaniel trotted into the drawing room, its pink tongue hanging out and its feathery tail waving wildly.

"Sit, Flora," commanded Lady Hurstwood, and the dog flopped down at her feet.

Another spaniel ran into the room, followed by a tall, thin man with wispy sandy hair and a harassed expression. He wore muddy corduroy trousers and boots, and a torn tweed jacket over a checked shirt. What was he doing in Lady Hurstwood's drawing room?

Lady Hurstwood said something to him that I couldn't understand, but from her looks and gestures, I think she was telling him off about his muddy boots. Then she said, "Anna, this is my husband, Charles."

Her husband?

This scruffy man, dressed like a tramp, was Lord Hurstwood, the owner of Ashcombe Park?

England was very confusing.

Lady Hurstwood was talking to her husband. She spoke fast and I couldn't follow what she said. Then Lord Hurstwood turned to me.

"I'm very sorry to hear about your situation, Anna. Dreadful business. Appalling man."

"But don't worry any more," Lady Hurstwood said. "We have work in the kitchens, if that would suit your mother. And outdoor work for your father."

My heart beat wildly. Had they really said what I thought they'd said?

"Johnny could do with a hand in the stables," said Lord Hurstwood. "Especially if that wretched man does bring us all to war. The youngsters will all join up and then we'll need all the help we can get. Could your father work with horses?"

I didn't understand all of this. But I understood his question.

I pictured my father, pale and stooped from sitting at a desk all day. He must once have been fit and strong. He had won the Iron Cross, after all. But now?

Had he ever even touched a horse?

"Of course," I said. "He loves horses."

"Excellent," said Lord Hurstwood. "That's all settled then."

"Don't worry about anything, Anna," said Lady Hurstwood, taking my hands and squeezing them. "Just give us your parents' details and we'll do the rest."

Could this really be happening?

She handed me a notepad and pen. In a daze, I wrote down the details she asked for: my parents' names, address and dates of birth.

As we walked home, down the front drive this

time, through the avenue of chestnut trees, I realised I'd been so overwhelmed that I hadn't even thanked them.

"Don't worry," said Molly. "I thanked them for you."

When I wrote to my parents that night with the news, I was happier than I could ever remember being in my whole life. The only thing worrying me was whether Lord and Lady Hurstwood would keep their promises. It all seemed too easy, too good to be true.

But they did keep their promises. I received a joyful letter from my mother the following week, saying that Lady Hurstwood had written to her on the very same day we had visited Ashcombe House.

"Papa and I are *so* happy, my darling, and so very, *very* proud of you for making this miracle happen," she wrote. "After the terrible sadness and despair we've felt for so many months, this lightness and joy is extraordinary. Every day, I wake up and laugh with sheer delight at the thought that soon we will be with you in England."

I felt the same. My only worry now was that the Nazis wouldn't grant them visas. But at the end of August Mama wrote with the amazing news that they had their visas! They just needed to get one last document stamped, and then they would be travelling to England the very next week! They were to have a married couple's apartment in Ashcombe House, and we would all be together, all three of us living in this magical place.

I couldn't wait to show them the village and the Park, and for them to meet my foster family. I wrote and asked them to bring the rest of my drawing pencils and as much paper as they could. Aunty Rose asked me about their favourite foods and planned a welcome meal. I helped clean the cottage and picked plums and damsons for preserving. It was beautiful weather and I lived in a bubble of happiness. When worries about their journey or the rumours of imminent war crept into my head, I pushed them firmly away. I was determined to stay in my bubble.

And then the bubble burst.

On 1st September, Germany invaded Poland. On 3rd September, Britain declared war on Germany.

My parents were now classed as "enemy nationals". The British government immediately cancelled their visas. No Germans could travel to Britain any more.

My parents were trapped.

CHAPTER TWENTY

Probably
a Spy

I cried for days. I was in a pit so deep and dark that nothing and nobody could reach me. I thought I would die of grief.

I cried from desolation at the shattering of my hopes and dreams. I cried from anger. How could the British government be so stupid, so heartless? I cried from fear and worry. What would happen to my parents now? And I cried from sheer aching homesickness. I felt as an actual physical pain the space between me and my parents growing wider and wider. And I was terrified that eventually they would be so far away that I wouldn't be able to reach them any more.

In the end, it was my anger at the British government that spurred me to stop crying and take action. I wrote to the Prime Minister, Neville Chamberlain, to explain my parents' situation and tell him exactly why his policy was so stupid. Molly corrected my grammar and I posted the letter.

Once I'd done that, my natural optimism started to return. Perhaps the government would see sense and realise the obvious truth that German Jews were not on Hitler's side. Even if they didn't change their policy, perhaps Mr Chamberlain would make an exception for my parents once he'd read my letter. Or, if that didn't happen, perhaps my parents would somehow manage to escape and come to England.

These few glimmers of hope were enough to give me the strength I needed to smile and put on a brave face when the autumn term started and I walked to the village school with Molly and Frank for the first time.

We called for some of their friends at the cottages we passed, and we met others walking along the way. I'd already met most of them during the summer holidays and they were all friendly. Walking to school that morning, it felt nice to be a part of a group again.

Most of the conversation was about the London evacuees that lots of the other children had staying with them. They had arrived last week with their teacher, who was staying with the vicar and his wife. The evacuees were going to have the village hall for their school, but it wouldn't be ready until tomorrow, so they had an extra day's holiday.

"Lucky things," said Nancy, who hated school.

"It's not going to be much of a holiday for our one," said Dorothy. "Mum's got her cleaning and polishing all day. I'd rather be at school."

"Ours just cries for his mummy," said Margaret. "And he wets the bed every night. Poor little thing, he's only three. I tried reading him a story to cheer him up, but he snatched the book out of my hand and threw it on the floor."

Since it was the start of the school year, the smallest children were starting for the very first time, and some of them were clinging to their mothers and weeping at the school gate. In Germany there was a tradition that children were given a big paper cone filled with sweets to take to school on their first day, but that didn't seem to happen here, which was a shame. A cone full of sweets might have cheered them up.

Everybody milled about in the playground, chatting or playing games, until a teacher walked out of the building, ringing a bell that she held in her hand. The heaving mass formed itself into four straggly lines.

"Just stand with me for the moment," said Molly. "I expect you'll be in my class anyway."

She pointed out her teacher, Miss Marshall, who was also the headmistress. She was a tall, serious-looking woman with round glasses. Her cropped wavy hair was a faded brown, sprinkled with grey.

"Is she nice?" I whispered.

"She's nice if you work hard."

I studied Miss Marshall's face as we waited in line. Her eyes roamed over all the classes until they lit on a little girl in the youngest class, who was trying to contain her sobs by stuffing her fist into her mouth. Miss Marshall went and knelt beside her, and her serious expression turned into the loveliest smile.

I will work hard, I vowed to myself. I will work

hard and impress Miss Marshall.

But, to my great disappointment, I wasn't in Miss Marshall's class. As the younger children filed into the building, Miss Marshall's eyes came to rest on me. She walked over to me.

"Welcome, Anna," she said, with that kind smile again. "We are very pleased to have you here."

"Thank you, Miss Marshall."

"Now, I've had a talk with Mrs Dean," she said, to my surprise. Aunty Rose hadn't mentioned this. "She says your English is coming on remarkably well. I was going to suggest that you worked with the upper infants at first but, given how quickly Mrs Dean says you're progressing, I'm going to put you with the lower juniors."

She must have seen the disappointment in my face, because she said, "Don't worry, Anna. It's only while your English catches up with the others of your age. I have a feeling you'll be in the top class in no time at all."

The school was in an old building. The classrooms had high ceilings, and windows right at the top of the walls, too high to see out of. My teacher was called Miss Ambrose. She had droopy hair and wore droopy clothes, and she taught our lessons in a droopy way, as though she was too tired or uninterested to show any enthusiasm. Several of the children were chatting and messing about, and she either didn't notice or didn't care.

I wished I was in Miss Marshall's class. I made

up my mind that I would improve my English very quickly.

The children in the lower juniors were very interested in me. At morning break, when we were all given a little bottle of tepid milk to drink in the playground, they crowded round me, asking questions.

"How old are you? Aren't you too old for our class?"

"Margaret says you're German. Are you?"

"Why did you come to England? I thought the Germans hated the English."

"Say something in German."

That was a very popular suggestion. Several of the others begged me to say something in German. When I obliged, and told them my name and where I came from, they were enthralled.

"It sounds so funny! What does it mean?"

"Say it again."

"Say some more German. Teach us to count to ten."

So I taught them the German numbers up to ten, which they found hilarious.

"Aren't you going to drink your milk?" asked a boy called Alfie, who had said nothing up to this point.

The bottle was warm from sitting in the classroom all morning, and the milk had a thick layer of cream on the top. I wasn't keen on milk at the best of times, and creamy lukewarm milk was the worst. I handed it gratefully to Alfie, who took it with delight.

"Did you ever see Hitler?" asked Janet.

I shook my head.

"Hitler's crazy," said Stanley. "My mum says he's a madman and he won't stop until he's conquered the world."

"Well, he won't conquer the world, will he?" said Barbara. "Because we're going to smash him to pieces."

"Sidney's really good at Hitler," said Janet. "Do Hitler, Sidney."

Excited faces turned to Sidney.

"Oh, yes, do old Hitler, Sid!"

"Go on, Sidney, show her your Hitler!"

Sidney spat on his hand and slicked down the front of his hair. Then he put one finger under his nose for a moustache and started goose-stepping around the playground, screaming and ranting in a stream of nonsense words. The other children were laughing and egging him on, but my stomach was squirming and I found myself darting frightened glances around the playground.

Don't be ridiculous, I told myself. It's all right to mock Hitler here. Nobody will mind.

A crowd had gathered round Sidney. I was filled with envy as I looked at their laughing faces. How wonderful it would be to see Hitler as a figure of fun.

"What's wrong with you, German girl?"

My stomach clenched. There was an edge to the question. I looked to see who had spoken.

"Don't you like people making fun of Hitler? Are you on his side then?"

It was a short, stocky boy from Molly's class. He had a freckled face and curly brown hair. He took a step towards me.

"My dad says the only good German is a dead German," he said.

I felt sick.

"Shut up, Billy," said Molly. "You know nothing."

"I know my dad's out in France, fighting the Germans. So what have you got one of them living in your house for? She's probably a spy."

Nancy gave a scornful laugh. "A spy? Don't be daft. She's twelve."

"Exactly. No one would ever suspect her. I bet she's been sent over specially by Hitler."

"I hate Hitler," I said.

"Well, you would say that, wouldn't you?"

The bell rang for the end of break and everyone filed back into the building. I walked inside with the others. But I felt as though I was six years old again, in the playground of my school in Germany.

I'd been playing with my friends when an older girl strode over and smacked me hard on the side of my face.

"Dirty Jew," she hissed, and while I was standing there in shock, she leaned forward and spat in my eye.

"My father told me to do that," she said, and walked away.

I was too shocked to cry. Ingrid and Ursula comforted me while I got out my handkerchief and wiped my face. But Irmgard had moved back a few paces. She was staring at me.

"You're not really Jewish, are you?" she said. "You never said you were a Jew."

Suddenly I felt frightened.

"No," I said. "I'm not Jewish."

I felt terrible as soon as I'd said it. And completely confused. Why was it bad to be Jewish?

I asked my parents the same question that evening, when I told them what had happened.

"Hitler is poisoning people's minds at the moment," said Mama, sitting me on her lap and kissing my cheek. "Many people are very poor, and they want somebody to blame. And Hitler is telling them the reason they're poor is because of the Jews. It's all lies, but some people are willing to believe it."

"It won't last," said Papa. "People will realise Hitler's a madman, and they'll turn against him. Things will soon be back to normal."

"But what about that horrible girl?" I said.

Mama held me tight. "I'll speak to your teacher tomorrow. She'll make sure it doesn't happen again."

Now, as I sat back down at my desk with the eight-year-olds, I felt cold with fear. Were Billy's comments just the beginning? Could what happened in Germany happen here too?

CHAPTER TWENTY-ONE

So Far
Away

Time passed.

It passed in air raid practices and gas mask drills, as we trained for a war in which nothing much actually seemed to be happening.

It passed in evenings when I read and reread my parents' letters and cried myself to sleep from homesickness, despite Clover doing her best to comfort me with her reassuring purrs.

It passed in school lunches eaten at our desks covered with greaseproof paper, instead of going home for lunch as we did in Germany. It passed in knitting socks for soldiers while Miss Ambrose read to us from *The Railway Children* and *The Land of Green Ginger*. In digging for victory in the school garden, sowing onions and cabbages, leeks and broad beans. In improving my English, helped by the kindness of Miss Marshall, who kept pace with my learning and lent me books from her own home. "I think you might like this," she would say, placing *Alice in Wonderland* or *The Secret Garden* on my desk when she came in to look at the lower juniors' work.

One day Miss Marshall asked me a question that nobody had asked me before.

"What do you enjoy, Anna? What sorts of things did you like to do at home?"

When I told her I used to play the piano, she said I could come to her house after school any time I wanted to and practise on hers. The piano was in the front room of her cottage, just down the lane from school. On warm autumn days, she kept the window open, and sometimes I would look up from playing to see a group of my schoolmates standing outside, listening.

The seasons passed too. The dusty roads and golden wheat fields of August gave way to dewy mornings and spiders' webs, autumn leaves and fat brown conkers, each one a shining treasure to be unwrapped from its spiky green casing, only to fade within days to a disappointing dullness. I learned the names of the jewel-like berries that glowed in the hedgerows: rosehips and haws, blackberries and sloes.

Christmas came, with holly cut from the hedgerows, a tree cut from the woods and paper snowflakes cut from newspaper, strung on the cottage windowpanes with threads of cotton. In my stocking – an old wool sock of Uncle Bert's – I found a bar of chocolate, a tangerine and a pink sugar mouse. Best of all, I found a box of drawing pencils and a book called *Ballet Shoes*, about three orphaned girls who have to make their own way in the world. I loved that book.

Then came the terrible bitter cold of January,

February and March, when we all huddled round the kitchen table in the warmth of the Rayburn stove, dreading the time when we had to take hot-water bottles to unheated bedrooms, where the icy wind blew through the gaps around the draughty windows.

And then came signs of spring, with flowers whose English names I learned and loved. First the snowdrops and daffodils poked their way up through the frozen earth, then celandines, wood anemones and primroses, while the hedgerows bloomed with blackthorn blossom.

I met Miss Marshall in the lane one day, when I was walking to the shops on an errand for Aunty Rose. I had crouched down to examine a cluster of primroses, thinking I would like to draw them but I didn't have a pencil in the right shade of yellow.

"Such a comfort, nature, isn't it?" Miss Marshall said. "The way it just does its own thing, to its own rhythms, regardless of the hideous mess we humans are making of the world. I do find it reassuring that, however bad the news may be, the trees still come into leaf and the flowers into bloom."

Since the outbreak of war, there had been no post between England and Germany. There were only Red Cross letters. You were allowed to write a maximum of twenty-five words, and only family news, nothing political or related to the war. It was better than nothing, but only just.

Now that I couldn't write long letters to my parents any more, I started to keep a diary. It helped to have a place where I could write down my thoughts and feelings, and writing them down helped me organise them in my mind a little better. I still kept the box in my head locked up tightly though. There were some thoughts I couldn't write down.

I tried not to think too much about what life might be like for my parents, but there was a constant knot of worry inside me, which only loosened slightly when a Red Cross letter arrived. Only very slightly, though, because letters had to be sent via the Red Cross headquarters in Switzerland, so they took weeks or even months to get to me. I knew my parents had been all right when they sent the letter. But were they still safe now?

In bed in the blackout, trying to stave off the worries and the nightmares, I would fantasise that they had somehow managed to leave Germany and were on their way to me right now. I imagined them walking into the cottage kitchen as we were eating breakfast, or appearing in the school playground, or coming down the village lane towards me.

One drizzly grey afternoon in March, I was walking home from school with Molly and Frank as usual. We passed the blacksmith's forge just as the bus from Castlebridge drew up on the other side of the road. The passengers spilled out, and there, in the jumble of raincoats and hats and umbrellas and shopping baskets, I saw my mother, in her dark-green coat. My heart somersaulted. I gasped and dashed across the road, narrowly missing a bicycle that swerved to avoid me.

"Look where you're going, idiot!" shouted the cyclist, glaring over his shoulder.

I didn't care. I dodged my way through the throng at the bus stop.

"Mama! Mama!"

The woman in the green coat turned round.

She wasn't my mother. She was just an English woman in a green coat.

Everybody else turned round too. One woman said hello to me. I ignored her. My eyes were so blurred with tears that I could barely see. I stumbled back across the road. I didn't look at Molly and Frank, but I knew they were staring at me. I walked on in front of them, my head to the ground.

Molly ran to catch up with me. "Are you all right, Anna?"

I couldn't speak.

"Did you think you saw your mum?"

I nodded. She walked along beside me for a while in silence. Then she put her hand on my arm.

"It must be horrible, being so far away from them."

I quickened my pace. "I don't want to talk about it."

"All right."

She said nothing more, and we continued in silence. After a while, she slowed her pace until she was walking with Frank again, and I was stomping ahead of them, head down in the chill March drizzle.

CHAPTER TWENTY-TWO

A Perfect
New Daughter

One morning in April, Miss Ambrose handed back my essay on the Battle of Hastings and said, "I think you're ready to move up to the top class, Anna."

I glowed with pride as I carried my things to the empty desk next to Dorothy's at the back of Miss Marshall's classroom. I was in the top class at last!

But then I glanced at Molly and saw the frown on her face. She caught my eye and gave me a smile and a thumbs-up sign. But I had seen her real reaction, and the warm feeling had disappeared.

After tea that evening, Aunty Rose went to get ready for her WI meeting, and Uncle Bert and Frank went out to work in the garden. Molly sat at the kitchen table to do her homework. I fetched the broom from the scullery to sweep the kitchen.

"Oh, you are good, Anna," said Aunty Rose, as she pulled her coat off the peg in the hall. "Thank you so much."

The front door closed behind her. Molly looked up from her book and said, "I wish you'd stop being such a goody-goody."

I stopped sweeping and looked at her.

"What do you mean? What is a goody-goody?"

Molly gave an impatient sigh. "You know, always helping around the house, doing everything you're told the second you're asked to do it." She put on a silly voice. "'Let me do that, Aunty Rose. How can I help you, Aunty Rose?' It's really annoying. You're showing me up."

"Showing you up?"

"Making me look lazy. I do all my chores, but now you come along and start doing all this extra stuff, actually offering to do more jobs all the time. And on top of that, working really hard at school, and playing the piano, and everyone knows you're Miss Marshall's favourite. I can see Mum and Dad looking at me like they're disappointed with me. Like now they've got a perfect new daughter and I'm not good enough for them any more."

"Oh, no!" I said, horrified. "I just like to help your parents, because they're so good to me. It's the only way I can repay them for their kindness. And also..."

I wasn't sure I wanted to say it.

"Also what?" asked Molly irritably.

"Also, because I like to be busy. It helps me not to think about ... things."

"Oh," said Molly, looking slightly ashamed. "Well, just be a bit less eager to please, can't you? It's annoying."

I nodded dumbly. "All right."

"Well, don't look so upset. It's nothing to get upset about."

And she turned back to her homework.

I felt as though she'd hit me. The last thing I'd wanted to do was upset her. I wanted to shout: *I don't want to be their daughter! I have my own parents! I didn't want to live with a strange family in a strange country. I'm just trying to make the best of it!*

But that would sound ungrateful and rude.

How would I feel if I were in Molly's position? If my parents had taken in a refugee child and showered them with such generous love and affection? I'd probably have felt exactly the same as she did.

So after that I tried to help a bit less around the house. It was horrible. Whenever Aunty Rose mentioned a job that needed doing, I would instinctively say, "I'll do it," and then I would catch Molly's glare from the other side of the table. I'd either do the job and face her annoyance, or make up a reason why I couldn't do it after all, and feel terrible. It felt like walking a tightrope, and it gave me a permanent stomach ache.

But though I might try to do a bit less housework to spare Molly's feelings, there was no way I was going to try less hard with my schoolwork. In my next Red Cross letter, I told my parents I was now in the top class. I knew how happy that would make them. I had promised them I'd make the most of every opportunity I was given, and there was no way I was going to break that promise.

CHAPTER TWENTY-THREE

The Ashcombe
Anti-German League

We'd been expecting air raids and bombing as soon as war was declared. Uncle Bert built an Anderson shelter in the garden and made it quite cosy inside. But for some reason nothing much happened for months and months and months.

Then one morning in April 1940 I came down for breakfast and saw the headline in Uncle Bert's newspaper. "Hitler Invades Norway and Denmark!"

I turned cold. He was coming closer. What would happen now?

But, once again, nothing much did seem to happen. Troops were sent to Norway, and there were naval battles, but it never really seemed clear which side was winning. Denmark was under Nazi control though. I tried to avoid hearing the news. After all, I could do nothing about it, and hearing about Nazi victories only gave me nightmares. When the wireless was switched on, I left the room if I could, and went upstairs to read. If I was helping in the kitchen and couldn't get away, I recited times tables in my head to drown out the announcer's voice.

Anyway, Norway and Denmark were a long way away.

But then, in May, Germany invaded Holland and Belgium overnight. When we heard the news on the wireless the next morning I felt paralysed with terror.

"All those poor, poor people," said Aunty Rose. "Their lives ruined, and all for a few madmen hell-bent on world domination."

What would happen to the lovely Dutch ladies at the train station? Had they been Jewish too? Thank goodness I had managed to bring Ezra to England. I wondered where he was now. He must have grown so much. He might even be walking. He would think his foster parents were his real parents. When his mother came to fetch him after the war, she would be a stranger to him.

Winston Churchill took over from Neville Chamberlain as Prime Minister, which pleased everybody.

"He's a proper leader," said Uncle Bert. "Old Hitler won't be able to get away with anything now Winston's in charge, you wait and see."

But even Churchill didn't seem to be able to stop the Nazis. The Dutch surrendered after only a few days, and then it got even worse.

The Germans invaded France.

France! What if they reached Paris? Where was Uncle Paul now? Would the Nazis find him? And what would they do to him if they did?

I tried to push the thoughts out of my mind, but

it was impossible when all the talk in the school playground was about the Germans invading us by parachute.

"They dropped into Holland in the dead of night, wearing Dutch and British army uniforms," said Ernie Hibbert. "Thousands of them, all disguised as British and Dutch soldiers."

"My nan says they're going to land all over England disguised as nuns," said Margaret. "If you see a nun, check what she's wearing on her feet. They have army boots on under their habits, she says. That's what gives them away."

"Sometimes they come disguised as vicars," said Nancy. "You can't trust no one no more."

"You can trust our vicar," said Dorothy. "He's been here years and years."

Nancy rolled her eyes. "I wasn't talking about *him*. I mean newcomers. Strangers."

"Like her," said Billy Townsend, pointing to me.

Everyone's eyes turned on me.

"In Holland," said Billy, "there were all these Germans what'd been living in Holland for years and years, good as gold. No one had a clue they were secretly Nazis all along. And when the German parachutists landed, these Germans all came rushing out to help them take over Holland. I read it in the paper. That's why Churchill's rounded up all the Germans living over here. Sent them all to internment camps, so they can't help the parachutists when they come."

"Only if they're over sixteen," said Margaret. "It

said in the paper. All enemy aliens over the age of sixteen."

"Exactly!" said Billy, triumphantly. "It's just like I said. That's why Hitler's using schoolgirls for spies. No one ever suspects girls. I bet she's collecting information the whole time and sending it back to Hitler. Stanley said he saw her drawing the church the other day. What's she drawing the church for, except to send the drawing off to Hitler so as he can bomb it?"

"Don't be an idiot," said Molly. "If Hitler wants to bomb the church, he doesn't need Anna's drawing to help him. I'm sure Hitler knows what a church looks like."

"My dad's out in France fighting the Nazis," said Billy, "and he says he doesn't see why he should be risking his life to protect this country against the Germans when some German girl's allowed to live over here and go to our school and all the time she's sending information back to Hitler. I don't believe she's a refugee at all. She doesn't look like a refugee. She's not poor. Look at her clothes. And she can play the piano. Poor kids don't play the piano."

"I hate Hitler," I said, my stomach churning. "I had to leave my home because of Hitler."

Billy raised his eyebrows meaningfully. "I bet you did."

"What's that supposed to mean?" said Nancy.

"Nothing," said Billy. "I'm just saying, I bet Hitler was very happy for you to come over here and send information back to him. I bet that suited him just fine."

Everyone was looking at me. Even Molly didn't say anything. Nor did Nancy or Margaret or Dorothy.

"Churchill thinks he's sorted everything out," said Billy, "locking up all the Germans over sixteen, when there's kids like her allowed to live free, drawing targets and sending letters back to Germany full of secret information. I bet old Hitler's laughing his head off, fooling Churchill with that trick. But you don't fool me, German girl. I know what you're up to."

The bell rang for the end of break. I felt sick. My head throbbed and I couldn't think. Miss Marshall set us a comprehension on an extract from *Treasure Island*. I kept trying to read it, but the words were just meaningless marks on the page.

In the row in front of me, Billy was writing a lot more than usual. Every now and then he nudged Ernie and showed him what he'd written. Ernie nodded in approval, and sometimes he pointed to something on the page and whispered to Billy. Occasionally he turned and glanced at me.

I dropped my pencil over the front of my desk and leaned forward to pick it up, trying to read what Billy had written. Ernie nudged him and he covered the book with his arms.

But not before I'd seen my name written on the paper.

I sat at my desk, my head throbbing. At the end of the lesson, Billy tore the page out of his exercise book, folded it and put it in his pocket. At dinner time

I saw him showing it to people in the playground. Other people started looking at me suspiciously. I stayed with Molly, Nancy and Dorothy and he didn't come up to us, but I saw Margaret on the edge of a group huddled around Billy.

During afternoon lessons, there were a lot of whispered conversations going on. Margaret was whispering to Molly the whole time we were copying a map in geography. When I put my hand up to answer a question in arithmetic, the room went silent. Everybody was looking at me, scrutinising my face, listening intently. Even my friends. Even Molly.

Just before the end of school, I saw my chance. Billy took his jacket off and hung it on the back of his chair. A folded piece of paper stuck out of the pocket.

I dropped my pencil on the floor and ducked under my desk to retrieve it. As I picked it up with one hand, I pulled the piece of paper out of Billy's pocket with the other. Then I sat at my desk again, tucking it into the pocket of my dress.

Molly chatted away as usual on the walk home, but I had my hand on the folded paper the whole time and I barely heard a word she said. As soon as we got home, I went to the bottom of the garden, sat under the apple tree and unfolded it.

It was a list, in Billy's neatest handwriting.

The Ashcombe Anti-German League

Evidence For Anna being a German Spy

1. She's German.
2. She's a schoolgirl – perfect disguise, no one would suspect her.
3. She sends letters to Germany – probably coded messages to Hitler.
4. She gets letters from Germany, written in German. Probably coded instructions from her spymasters.
5. She's drawn pictures of places in Ashcombe and sent them to Germany – probably to help the German bombers find their targets.
6. She speaks nearly perfect English. Trying to pass as an English girl so she can spy for Germany without being suspected.
7. She reads English books. Probably trying to learn things about England to tell Hitler, so he can train other spies to act like English people.
8. She's quiet and very well behaved – trying to fit in and not cause suspicion.
9. She says she came to England because her family was being persecuted by Hitler, but how do we know? There's no evidence that she was persecuted. She brought fancy dresses and she can play the piano, so we know she's not poor.

Evidence Against Anna being a German Spy

None

CHAPTER TWENTY-FOUR

On the
Outside

Sitting there, reading that list, I felt completely alone in the world.

What could I do? Would Billy turn everyone against me? How could I defend myself? I couldn't prove that I wasn't a spy, so how could I convince them? And what if Churchill decided to intern Germans under sixteen too? Would I be taken away to a prison camp?

I stayed there until Aunty Rose called me in for tea. I was dreading facing them all and having to pretend to be normal.

But their attention was on other things. They had just heard on the BBC that the Germans had reached the port of Calais, on the French coast.

"Twenty miles away!" exclaimed Aunty Rose. "To think those evil men are only twenty miles from Kent. It doesn't seem possible."

I sat, frozen, ice-cold with terror.

Nowhere was safe any more.

Images flashed through my mind. Nazi jackboots marching through Ashcombe. Swastikas hanging from the flagpoles.

What would they do to me?

"Are you all right, Anna?" asked Aunty Rose. "You're white as a sheet. Don't you feel well?"

"No," I said. "I might go and lie down."

My legs shook when I stood up. I gripped the banister rail as I walked upstairs.

My heart raced and my head spun.

If the Nazis came, I would have to run. I wouldn't let them catch me and I couldn't get the Deans in trouble. I would go and hide in the woods.

No. They would search the woods with dogs and guns.

I would go to London. I had no money for the train fare but there must be ways to sneak on without paying. I could pretend to be an orphan. Somebody would look after me, surely.

Bloomsbury House! I would go to Bloomsbury House, where the Refugee Committee had their offices. One of those ladies would take care of me.

I pulled my little case from under my bed and packed my clothes, along with *Heidi* and *Ballet Shoes*. I looked at the box of my parents' letters on the bedside table. Molly would notice if that was gone. I would have to put it in the case at the last minute. I made a space for it at the side.

I slid the case back under the bed. My heart was still thumping, but I felt slightly calmer. At least I had a plan.

The next week at school was really horrible. People huddled in corners, whispering and shooting glances

121

in my direction. When I walked past them, they nudged each other and stared at me.

My friends still stuck by me though. At least, none of them said or did anything nasty, but I could tell they were thinking things they weren't telling me.

The war news was getting even worse. The Germans trapped the retreating British and French armies at Dunkirk, on the Normandy coast. As well as the Navy, lots of people were crossing the Channel in little boats to bring the soldiers home, and it seemed that everybody in the village was waiting for news of their men.

On Sunday afternoon, Aunty Rose asked me and Molly to go with her to visit Mrs Digweed, an elderly widow.

"Poor woman, both her sons are out in France and she's beside herself waiting for news," Aunty Rose said. "You two will be a nice distraction for her."

We took her some eggs and a jar of plum jam. As we drew near to the crossroads by the church and the war memorial, we saw the Air Raid Patrol warden and another man, Joe Thomas, digging a hole around the signpost.

"Gosh," said Molly. "They're doing it already."

We had heard on the news yesterday that the government had ordered every signpost in the country to be taken down, so if German parachutists landed, they wouldn't know where they were.

The warden took hold of the white-painted post

and wobbled it. It had four arms on the top, printed with the names of the neighbouring villages.

"That should do it, I reckon," he said to Mr Thomas. "Let's give it a go."

Mr Thomas straightened up and laid down his spade. Both men grasped the post and heaved it out of the ground.

"Hello, Mrs Dean," called a woman's voice. We turned to see Miss Marshall coming out of the church, carrying a stack of parish magazines.

We all said hello, and then Miss Marshall said, "I thought I'd better take these. There's not much point removing the signposts if a parachutist can just walk into the church and find the name of the village printed on the front of the magazine."

"Goodness, yes," said Aunty Rose. "I hadn't thought of that."

I shivered at the thought of a Nazi parachutist striding into the village church. Miss Marshall must have noticed, because she gave me a rather strained smile.

"Ignore me, Anna. I'm just being silly. I hope you're not worrying about all these rumours of parachutists and suchlike. People are getting a bit hysterical at the moment."

It didn't seem hysterical to me. It seemed completely realistic. How could Miss Marshall sound so calm? Didn't she know what would happen to her if the Germans invaded?

When I was nine, we had walked into our classroom one Monday morning to find a man in a black suit standing at the front. He held a cane in his hand. He told us he was our teacher now, and his name was Herr Molsen.

"But where's Frau Schmidt?" asked Klaus. We all liked Frau Schmidt. She was decent and fair, and she rarely used her cane. And after that girl had spat at me, Frau Schmidt had patrolled the playground every break time.

"Frau Schmidt has left the school," Herr Molsen said.

He wore a swastika badge on his jacket. He made me and Esther, the only other Jewish student, sit at the back of the classroom, with an empty row of desks between us and the other children, as though being Jewish was an infectious disease.

He told the class that every time he walked into the room, we must all stand up and raise our right arms in the Hitler salute. He demonstrated it, stabbing his right arm straight out in front of him, palm down.

"*Heil Hitler!*" he shouted.

"*Heil Hitler!*" shouted everyone except me and Esther. My stomach was jumping with nerves, but I kept my head down and my arms by my side. Papa had told me I never had to say those words.

Then I glanced up and caught Herr Molsen's eye. He was glaring at me with a look of such hatred that I shuddered and lowered my head again.

"You! You at the back! Raise your hands!"

To my astonishment, Esther slowly raised her hand.

"*Heil Hitler,*" she mumbled.

My mouth was dry. I was trembling with fear, petrified that Herr Molsen would stride across the classroom and strike me with his cane.

"Sit down," he said, "and take out your books."

I risked another glance at him.

He wasn't looking at me. I sat down and took out my book.

Herr Molsen never looked at me or spoke to me again. It was as though he had decided I didn't exist. And at break time that day, I discovered that the rest of the class had taken their cue from him. None of the other children, not even Ingrid, would play with me, speak to me or even look at me. They acted as though I was invisible. When I tried to speak to them, they simply turned their backs and carried on their conversations.

My parents could tell something was wrong but when they asked me I said everything was fine. I didn't want to make them more worried than they already were.

Now I looked at Miss Marshall, talking to Aunty Rose. Did she realise that if the Germans invaded she would be replaced by a teacher who would turn all the children into Nazis?

"I'm glad I've seen you, Mrs Dean," she said. "I wanted to let you know how wonderfully Anna's getting on at school. Her progress is really remarkable. Her English is almost flawless, and she's doing superbly in her other subjects too."

I didn't dare glance at Molly. *I never asked for*

praise, I wanted to tell her. *I just want to learn.*

"Molly's doing extremely well too," said Miss Marshall, to my great relief. "I'm very keen that both of them try for a scholarship to the grammar school next year. They're such bright girls, it would be a terrible waste of their potential to leave school at fourteen."

"Oh, well," said Aunty Rose uncomfortably. "I'm not sure. Isn't the uniform very expensive? And then there's all the books they'd need."

"I'm sure there's something we could do about that. I'll have a think. Perhaps Bloomsbury House might be able to help with Anna's expenses."

"I don't know," said Aunty Rose. "They don't seem to have a lot of money for luxuries."

"Education isn't a luxury, Mrs Dean," said Miss Marshall.

"Maybe, but fancy uniforms and Latin textbooks certainly feel like luxuries when your children are wearing shoes they've grown out of and you've no idea how you're going to afford new ones for the winter."

"Yes, of course," said Miss Marshall. "I'm sorry. I didn't mean to cause offence."

"None taken," said Aunty Rose, forcing a smile. "You're just doing your job. And it's lovely to hear how well the girls are doing."

But her face was clouded over as we walked to Mrs Digweed's house.

Mrs Digweed had just had a postcard from her younger son to say he was safely back in England

and would be coming to see her next week. Her happiness cheered us all up, and we left her with hopeful assurances that she would be bound to hear from her other boy very soon.

As we walked back, we saw the greengrocer outside his shop, balanced precariously at the top of a ladder. He was painting out the village name on his sign. Now it just said _____ Greengrocers. We looked at the neighbouring shops and saw that their signs had been changed in the same way. Ashcombe General Stores was now _____ General Stores and Ashcombe Bakery was _____ Bakery.

"Them parachutists won't have a clue where they are if they land in our fields now," he said triumphantly, as we passed his ladder.

"He seems to think he's outwitted Hitler all by himself," muttered Aunty Rose, when we were out of earshot. "I think it might take a bit more than Will Eaves and a paintbrush to stop a Nazi invasion."

That evening, as always, while Clover sat purring on my lap, I opened my box of letters.

I always kept them in order, with the most recent one on top. But tonight the letter at the top of the pile was one from several months ago.

That was very strange.

I took them all out and checked through them. A few of the others were in the wrong places too. I put them back in order and counted them. They were all there.

Had I accidentally put them back in the wrong order last night? Or ... had somebody else been rummaging through the box?

CHAPTER TWENTY-FIVE

Betrayed

When everybody filed into the classroom on Monday morning, I saw Billy go up to Molly's desk and whisper something. I couldn't make out his words or her reply, but I saw them both glance surreptitiously at me. I averted my eyes and sat down miserably at my desk.

The morning passed in the same way all recent mornings had passed. Dorothy was the only person who still treated me exactly as she always had. Thank goodness we shared a desk.

At playtime, after I had given away the disgusting bottle of tepid milk, Dorothy and I went to the garden. We had arranged to meet all the garden monitors there, but nobody else turned up, so we swept out the shed and neither of us mentioned the fact that the others hadn't come.

After break, Miss Marshall set us yet another comprehension exercise. Just as we were about to start, Miss Carragher, the infants teacher, came in and said something to her.

"Get on with your work, everybody," said Miss Marshall. "I'm just popping over to the infants."

The comprehension passage was an extract of a poem called *Hiawatha*. I loved the rhythm of it.

Something in the hazy distance,
Something in the mists of morning,
Loomed and lifted from the water,
Now seemed floating, now seemed flying,
Coming nearer, nearer, nearer.

With the teacher gone, the noise level grew and grew. I tried to lose myself in the poem, but people were getting out of their seats and milling around, and I gradually became aware of a group gathered in front of Miss Marshall's desk. Molly was there, and so was Nancy.

They were craning their heads to read a piece of paper that Billy was holding. They were staring at it, whispering and darting glances at me.

Had Billy written another list, accusing me of more treachery?

I caught Molly's eye. She flushed guiltily. Billy caught my eye too, and shoved the paper at Molly. As it changed hands, I saw the handwriting.

My mother's handwriting.

For a moment I sat there, disbelieving. Then, boiling with rage, I sprang out of my seat, dashed up the aisle and snatched the letter from Molly.

"You traitor!" I screamed. "You evil thief! How dare you? How *dare* you go through my private things? My only things, my precious things, the only things I have from my parents! How dare you?

How could you?"

Molly's face was white. Her eyes were huge and terrified. The room was utterly silent. The class held its breath.

"Miss Marshall's coming!" somebody hissed.

Everyone scurried to their seats. When Miss Marshall walked back in, I was bending silently over my books like everybody else. But inside, I was a boiling cauldron of rage and hurt.

I didn't speak for the rest of the morning. Dorothy whispered, "Are you all right?" and I nodded. Apart from that, I had no communication with anybody.

When we were dismissed after dinner, I headed towards the big elm tree in the far corner of the school field.

"Anna, wait!"

It was Molly. I kept my head down and quickened my pace.

"Anna, please wait."

"Go away."

"Please, just let me talk to you."

"Leave me alone."

I reached the tree. It grew right next to the fence. There was nowhere to go from here.

Molly caught up with me. She reached out for my arm. I shook her hand away.

"Get off me."

"Anna, please. I'm so sorry."

I glanced at her face and saw, to my surprise, that she had tears in her eyes.

"I'm so sorry. I was such an idiot. I should never

131

have taken that letter. It's just… It was Billy. He just kept on and on about you being a spy, and he had all these reasons, and I thought, well, we don't have any actual evidence that you're not."

A sound came out of my mouth: a harsh, explosive sound.

She hurried on. "He said it was my patriotic duty to bring in one of your letters, just in case. So he could look at it and see if it was in code. He said he knew how to decipher codes. I told him you weren't a spy, but he said it couldn't do any harm just to check, and I owed it to my country not to take any chances. I'm so sorry. It all sounds so stupid now. I should never have taken any notice of him. He was just… He just kept going on and on, and I… I was an idiot."

I looked at her pathetic, tearful face, and my boiling anger and hurt turned into cold, hard hatred.

"I'm finished with you, Molly Dean. You've done the worst thing you could possibly have done, and you know it. You know how much those letters mean to me. You know they're all I have from my parents. But you just don't care."

"I do care. I just—"

"You probably enjoyed doing it. It probably made you feel important. You've never really wanted me here, have you? You pretended to be so friendly and helpful and nice, but you've always secretly resented me. You don't like it when I do well at school. You even accused me of trying to steal your parents. As if I would want to do that! I have my own parents!

All I've ever wanted is to live with them. And why on earth would I want to help Hitler? You know Hitler hates Jews. You know he put my father in a concentration camp. Why would I be on his side? You're as bad as Billy. You're as bad as the Nazis. You're a horrible person and I'm never going to speak to you again."

Molly was sobbing now, tears streaming down her face.

"Please, Anna. Please, please forgive me. I'm so sorry, I truly am."

"I will never forgive you, Molly Dean," I said. "Never. Not for as long as I live."

CHAPTER TWENTY-SIX

If the
Invader Comes

After what Molly had done, I wasn't going to pander to her by helping less in the house. I made sure I was occupied for every moment of every day. I also started going to bed early with a book. When I heard Molly coming upstairs, I would lie down and pretend to be asleep, so I didn't have to speak to her. I left the house earlier in the mornings, telling Aunty Rose I'd been made a classroom monitor and had duties before school.

I still walked home with Molly and Frank, but only because I didn't want Frank to know anything was wrong. He would chat away about his day and he didn't notice that I would just talk to him and never say a word to his sister.

Molly was making a big effort to be nice, always approaching me cautiously, as though I was a mistreated dog who might attack at the slightest provocation. I ignored her as much as possible without making things obvious to the rest of the family. I avoided eye contact and only spoke to her when I absolutely had to.

Everyone else at school was being extra chatty and

friendly. My friends all apologised for taking any notice of Billy. Nancy even wrote a letter begging my forgiveness, and Margaret baked me a cake.

It wasn't too hard to forgive them. They'd been friendly to me from the beginning, and they had resisted all Billy's nasty comments until the whole country became obsessed with spies and parachutists.

But I could never, ever forgive Molly.

Normally, Aunty Rose and Uncle Bert might have noticed something was wrong. But they had just been told that Lord and Lady Hurstwood were moving to Canada for the duration of the war, and their butler, Mr Robins, who was a friend of Uncle Bert's, had asked Uncle Bert and Aunty Rose to help the few remaining servants pack up the valuables and put the best furniture into storage. (It was Mr Robins, I discovered, whom I'd mistaken for Lord Hurstwood, when Molly and I had gone to Ashcombe House to ask for jobs for my parents.)

So the days passed, and outwardly things seemed much the same as before.

And then, one morning in the middle of June, everything changed again.

We had just finished breakfast when we heard a vehicle rumbling up the lane. Frank ran into the front room and looked out of the window.

He turned to us, grinning, his cheeks flushed with excitement. "An army truck! Coming into the yard!"

The truck drove across the yard and stopped right outside the cottage. The vehicle's doors opened and shut. Boots thudded on the ground. My stomach knotted. There was a sharp knock at the door. I felt sick. Every sight of a soldier, every knock on the door still had that effect on me.

Aunty Rose opened the door. Filling the little doorway stood an officer and a soldier, both in khaki battledress.

"Good morning, madam," said the officer. "I'm sorry to disturb you, but we need to see what spare accommodation you have."

Aunty Rose laughed. "Chance would be a fine thing. We have two small bedrooms and five of us living here."

"All the same, we have to look, if you don't mind," said the officer.

"You'd better come in then."

She stepped aside to let them enter.

"My son sleeps in here," she said, showing them the little front room, with Frank's bedding folded up on the sofa. The officer glanced inside and nodded.

She led him up the steep staircase. "The girls sleep here," she said, and I heard the creak of our bedroom door, followed by the rattle of the latch on the other side of the tiny landing. "And this is our room," she said. "My husband and I."

"I see," said the officer. "Well, you're right, there's no space to billet any soldiers. Thank you for your time, madam."

Nobody said anything until the truck started up again and left the yard. Then Aunty Rose said, "I wonder what that was about."

On the walk to school, everyone was talking

about the soldiers. It seemed they were visiting every house in the village, looking for spare bedrooms. They didn't have much luck. Everybody with a spare room had already taken in evacuees or land girls.

Rumours buzzed around school as to why the army was looking for accommodation. Two days later, Molly and I were getting dressed when we heard the rumbling of engines. Molly ran to the window and gasped.

"Army lorries. And motorbikes. Oh, my goodness, there's dozens of them!"

I stood frozen in terror. The Germans had come!

Molly rushed downstairs. I looked out of the window, my heart pounding.

A convoy of lorries, with motorcycle outriders, was making its way up the chestnut avenue towards Ashcombe House. It wasn't the German army. It was the British army.

What were they doing? Had the Germans invaded in the night?

I pulled the suitcase out from under my bed and packed the box of letters in it. Then I put my socks and shoes on as quickly as I could.

The back door opened. Had they come for me?

I picked up my case and was about to sprint down the stairs when Uncle Bert's voice stopped me in my tracks. So it wasn't the Nazis. Not yet. Just Uncle Bert, returning from his night shift with the Local Defence Volunteers.

I shoved the case back under the bed and walked downstairs, trying to look normal.

"Did you know about this?" Aunty Rose was asking, as I walked into the kitchen.

Uncle Bert laid his shotgun, tin hat and gas mask on the table. He looked tired, but his blue eyes were sparkling.

"I just heard, and then I almost got crushed by their blooming great convoy. The army's taking over the whole Park. Everyone with a spare room's having troops billeted on them, and the rest will be living in the big house."

Frank gasped with excitement. "Soldiers everywhere! Do you think they'll let me ride in their tanks?"

"They haven't got tanks," said Uncle Bert. "Not yet, at least. Trucks everywhere though, and lorries and motorbikes."

When we walked home from school that day, it was as though we were living in a different place. The entire Park had been transformed into an army camp. Everywhere there were soldiers, some being drilled, some exercising in vests and shorts, some servicing the vehicles that were parked all along the chestnut avenue and on the gravel in front of the main entrance. They said hello to us as we passed. Molly and Frank replied cheerily, Frank practically bouncing with excitement.

I tried to control my choking panic so I could say hello too. But my throat was too tight to speak.

The next day, Miss Marshall wasn't at her desk when we came in for afternoon lessons. She arrived five minutes late, which she had never done before.

She was very pale and her expression was strained. It was clear that she had something to say. We waited in silence.

"I am very sorry to have to tell you, children," she said, taking a deep breath, "that France has surrendered to Germany."

My body turned to ice.

There was nothing left. Nothing but the English Channel between us and Hitler.

The troops at Ashcombe Park, we learned, were stationed there as part of Britain's defences. The Germans were expected to invade the south coast at any moment. Everywhere, tank traps and pillboxes started to appear. All the beaches were mined and covered with barbed wire to repel invading troops. The government sent a leaflet to every household, called *If the Invader Comes*, with lots of instructions about staying in your home and not panicking. Aunty Rose was not impressed.

"Honestly!" she said, flinging the leaflet on the kitchen table. "Men! It's all very well telling everyone to refuse to give food or water to German troops, but what do they imagine a Nazi soldier's going to do if I try to stop him coming into my kitchen? And how is it going to help the war effort if my children end up motherless?"

Uncle Bert jerked his thumb towards the cupboard by the kitchen stove where his shotgun was locked up.

"If you see or hear anything suspicious when I'm

not around, Rosie, you get that gun out, all right? I'll be keeping it loaded and ready, and you know where the key is."

I knew where the key was too. But I had no idea how soon I would need that knowledge.

CHAPTER TWENTY-SEVEN

"The Germans Threaten to Invade Great Britain"

If the Invader Comes

On the last day of term, as Molly, Frank and I were walking home from school, Frank's chatter was drowned out by the wail of the air raid siren.

We stopped and looked at each other. We were on the long stretch of lane that led from the village centre to Ashcombe Park. There was nothing but fields on either side of us.

Terror forced me to speak to Molly.

"What should we do?"

"Wait and see."

The siren had sounded several times over the last few days, as German planes had started bombing British ports and shipping centres. Usually the air raid siren was followed almost immediately by the all-clear when the planes flew straight on towards their targets. But this noise was louder than usual. Two planes came into view, looming lower and larger.

"Get down!" yelled Molly, as a massive explosion almost deafened me. We dived into the ditch as another explosion shook the ground and the planes roared away.

We lay in the ditch, silent, trembling. My ears were ringing. Would there be more planes? Where had the explosions been? They sounded very close. Please, please let Aunty Rose and Uncle Bert be safe, I prayed over and over again.

After what seemed a very long time, Molly said, "Shall we get out?"

When we stood up, I saw I had scratches and nettle stings all over me. They hadn't hurt at all when we were in the ditch, but now they really stung.

"Let's get home," said Molly in a wobbly voice. I shot her a sideways glance. She was completely white. So was Frank.

"I think the bombs fell in the wood," I said. "They were probably aiming for the searchlight."

I was only guessing. I just wanted to reassure Frank. But the searchlight did seem a likely target. It was at the other end of the wood, about two miles away. I liked watching its beams as they roamed the night skies, looking for enemy planes. It made me feel safer to know the lights were searching the sky as we slept.

Molly broke into a run.

"Wait for me!" called Frank.

"Hurry up then." She reached for his hand and pulled him along. I ran a little way behind them.

"Mum?" Molly shouted, bursting through the back door. "Dad?"

Aunty Rose came running out of the kitchen. She threw her arms around all three of us.

"Oh, thank goodness you're safe!" she said,

squeezing us together.

"Where's Dad?" asked Molly.

"He's gone with the warden to see where the bombs fell. They reckon they were aiming for the searchlight."

When Uncle Bert came home, we learned that the bombs had missed the searchlight and exploded in the wood, creating a massive crater. The village was very lucky. Nobody was hurt and no houses were damaged.

Clover didn't appear for her supper that evening. I looked all over the house – under the beds, in the cupboards, behind the furniture – but there was no sign of her. I went into all the farm buildings to call her, but there was no response.

"Don't worry," said Aunty Rose. "You know she doesn't like loud noises. She'll be hiding somewhere quiet until she feels safe again. She'll come out when she's hungry."

But Clover still hadn't touched her food at breakfast time. I wanted to search for her, but Aunty Rose kept us busy all morning, and then Frank wanted me to work in the garden with him after lunch. By three o'clock, though, I couldn't stand the worry any more. What if Clover was injured, or stuck somewhere? I couldn't just do nothing. I had to search, and I wouldn't stop until I found her.

CHAPTER TWENTY-EIGHT

"Make Certain That No Suspicious Strangers Enter Your Premises"

If the Invader Comes

There was no sign of Clover in the stables, or the granary, or the pigsties, all places where she sometimes hunted for mice. I headed for the barn on the other side of the yard.

The huge door creaked as I pushed it open. A shaft of light streamed into the dark interior. Somebody gasped.

Molly and Frank were sitting on a hay bale by the wall, staring at the door. They looked terrified. Frank was gripping Molly's arm. When he saw me, he let out his breath in a sigh of relief.

"Oh, thank goodness it's you."

"What are you doing?" I asked.

Frank shot Molly a guilty glance.

"We thought we'd help look for Clover," said Molly. "Didn't we, Frank?"

Anger flared inside me. Molly was so obviously lying.

"And you thought you'd look for her by sitting on a bale?" I said.

They sprang to their feet.

"Clover!" called Molly, walking towards the

tangle of farm machinery in the far corner. "Clover, are you there?"

Frank hurried to a stack of empty grain sacks.

"Clover!" he called, lifting the top sack from the pile. "Clover, where are you?"

"Maybe she's in the loft," said Molly. "I'll go and look."

The hayloft was a wooden platform that ran along the width of the barn at the far end. Molly had her hand on the ladder when a voice said, "Excuse me?"

We froze. Frank stared at Molly, wide-eyed. It was a man's voice, and it seemed to have come from the loft.

"Excuse me," said the voice again. It definitely came from the loft. "I'm sorry if I've shocked you, but are you looking for a cat?"

We glanced at each other fearfully.

"Who are you?" called Molly. "Come down from there."

"I'm afraid I can't. I took shelter up here, but I've sprained my ankle and I can't walk. There's a black-and-white cat here. She's very friendly. Is she yours?"

"Clover!" I called. "Clover, come down!"

Clover mewed, but she didn't appear.

"Clover, go down," said the man coaxingly. "Go on."

Clover mewed again.

"I'm sorry," said the man. "She won't move and I can't move. You might have to come up and get her. I promise I won't bite."

He sounded friendly enough. But what was a

strange man doing in the hayloft?

"Let's all go," Molly mouthed to me silently.

I nodded. However much I despised her, I couldn't let her face the man alone.

"We're coming up," she called.

My heart thumped against my ribs as I climbed up behind her.

The loft had a small window at one side, which gave it a little more light than the rest of the barn. As I reached the top of the ladder, my throat tightened and my heart started racing as I saw a man in battledress, sitting with his legs stretched out in front of him, leaning against the end wall. Curled up next to him in a heap of straw was Clover.

I scooped her up and held her close to my chest, hoping her warmth would calm me.

"Clover," I murmured. "I've been so worried about you."

The soldier smiled at us. "So this is the cat you were looking for."

There were scratches and bloodstains on his face. He just had socks on his feet. His boots were beside him, next to his army haversack.

"I'm sorry if I shocked you," he said. "I was asleep, and then I was woken by your calling, and I guessed you must be looking for the cat. She's beautiful. And so friendly."

"Who are you?" asked Frank. "Are you one of the soldiers from the Park?"

"I am."

"But why are you in our barn? Why aren't you

with your regiment?"

"It's difficult to explain," said the man. "I am not sure you would understand."

"Of course we'd understand," said Molly indignantly. "We're not stupid."

The man looked at us for a moment. Then he said, "If I tell you, can I trust you not to tell anybody?"

Molly gave an outraged exclamation. "You've got a cheek. You're the one who's skulking around in our barn."

"Your barn?"

"Pretty much. My dad works on the estate and we live just over there."

"Even so," said the man, "it is difficult to tell you why I am here."

"Tell us," said Frank, who was clearly bursting with curiosity. "We can keep a secret. We won't tell anyone, will we, Molly?"

Molly screwed up her mouth and gave the man a hard look.

"All right. We won't tell anyone."

The man took a deep breath and paused for a few seconds, as if he didn't know how to begin. Then he said, "I have left my regiment, you see, and they might be looking for me."

Frank gasped. "You're a deserter?"

"No, no. I shall go back. But I need to visit my mother. I received a letter from her telling me that she is very ill. My father is dead and she has nobody to care for her. She lives in a remote cottage with no neighbours. I must go and see her and make arrangements for her to be cared for. I'm worried that if I do not do so, she may die."

"But wouldn't the army allow you to visit her, if she's really ill?" said Molly.

"It is a time of war. Things are not normal. I shall return as soon as I have made arrangements for my mother. But you can see that it is important for me to remain hidden."

Frank frowned. "But if you need to go and see your mother, why are you hiding in our barn?"

"That is the problem. I have injured myself. Look. I was running in the dark and I fell into a ditch."

He leaned forward and slowly pulled up his trouser leg. Then he rolled down his sock, wincing as he did so. I sucked in my breath. His ankle was swollen to twice the normal size, and covered in a huge purple bruise.

Frank looked stricken. "That must really hurt."

"So you see I cannot move at the moment," said the soldier.

Molly crouched down to get a better look. "That looks really nasty. We should call the doctor."

"No!" The words came out as a bark. Clover jumped out of my arms in shock. We stared at the man. He gave a forced smile.

"I apologise. But you will understand that I cannot see a doctor. He would be bound to report me to my commanding officer. I must just rest here until my ankle improves. I think it is sprained, not broken. In a few days, perhaps, I shall be able to walk on it."

"How did you get up to the loft?" asked Frank.

"I pulled myself up the ladder on one leg. I fell into the ditch just outside the farmyard. I lay in the ditch until it grew light, and then I saw this barn and crawled here. The pain was bad then, but it is worse now."

"You must be so hungry," said Molly, for whom lack of food was the most terrible calamity imaginable.

"I am very hungry, and also very thirsty."

"We can find you some food," said Frank. "Can't we, Molly?"

"I'm sure we can get you something," said Molly, "but we won't be able to take too much or Mum will notice. It would be a lot easier if we could tell her."

"No," said the man, shaking his head. "Don't tell your mother."

"She wouldn't report you, I'm sure. If she heard your story, she'd understand, the same as we do."

The man sounded as though he was choosing his words carefully.

"Your mother might not be as understanding as you children are. To many people, disobeying the order of one's superiors is a thing they would disapprove of. So, please, I would prefer it if you did not tell your parents. But if you could buy me some food, I would greatly appreciate it. I can pay."

He took a wallet from his pocket and handed Molly a pound note. I noticed a lot more notes in the wallet. Everyone said soldiers were well paid, but I hadn't realised they had that much money.

149

"Bread would be good, and butter if possible. And some cheese or ham. And cigarettes."

"Have you got your ration book?" asked Molly.

"Oh, how silly of me. No, I don't have it."

"We won't be able to get you the butter or ham then. And it's a bit late to go to the shops today. We'll get you some water now, and we can bring you some food from the house. Not too much, or Mum will notice, but enough for tonight. We'll go to the shops in the morning."

"Thank you," he said. "You are most kind."

"What's your name?" asked Frank.

"Peter," said the man. "Peter Smith."

"Goodbye, Peter Smith," said Frank. "We'll be back soon."

"Come on, Clover," I said. She was crouched by the wall, on her guard, but when I picked her up she settled happily into my arms and began to purr.

"She's a lovely cat," said the man.

I said nothing. We went down the ladder in silence. I handed Clover to Frank while I climbed down, and then took her back. It was so comforting to feel her warmth in my arms again.

None of us spoke or looked at each other until we were on the other side of the farmyard. I felt the tightness in my chest relax a little.

Frank hopped with excitement. "A real soldier in our barn!" he whispered. "And we're looking after him!"

"Shh," said Molly. "You promised not to say anything."

"But there's no one here. And I only whispered."

"Even so. You never know who might be around."

A sudden breeze made a stable door bang. Clover leapt out of my arms and raced back towards the barn. I ran after her.

"Just leave her," said Molly. "She'll come back when she wants to."

But I couldn't leave her. I needed her solid, comforting presence. And I didn't want her getting too friendly with Peter Smith, either. She was my cat. Not that I would have said that to Molly.

We had left the barn door slightly ajar, and I slipped through the gap. My plimsolls made no sound on the dirt floor.

I heard noises from the loft, as though the man was rummaging in his haversack.

He muttered to himself.

My stomach turned over.

No. It couldn't be. I must have heard wrong.

I stayed completely still, listening, my heart thumping. He was still rummaging, but he had stopped muttering.

Something rolled across the loft and dropped over the edge on to the barn floor. The man swore.

My blood froze in my veins.

He had sworn in German.

CHAPTER TWENTY-NINE

"Do Not Believe Rumours and Do Not Spread Them"

If the Invader Comes

My blood pounded in my ears. My legs felt weak.

It sounded as though the man was shuffling across the floor. I had to get away. I tiptoed out of the barn and sprinted across the yard, my heart pounding.

I caught up with the others just outside the cottage. I skidded to a stop, flailing my arms, and grabbed Frank's shoulder to steady myself.

"Ow," he said, pushing my hand away. "What are you doing?"

"Come to the tree house," I hissed.

Molly looked at me in surprise. Then her look turned to one of alarm.

"You're completely white. What's happened?"

"In the tree house. It's top secret."

I ran down the garden path and out through the little wooden gate at the bottom of the garden that led to the sheep field. I heard Molly and Frank following me.

I didn't stop until I reached the oak tree in the middle of the field. Then I turned slowly in a circle, scanning the horizon in all directions, trying to take deep breaths to stop my heart thudding against my ribcage.

There was nobody around.

We climbed the rope ladder to the tree house Uncle Bert had built. It wasn't really a house, just a plank platform with a low wooden wall around the edge. In winter, you could see for miles, but now the leaves formed a thick green canopy and we were completely hidden from view.

"Now, tell us everything," said Molly.

"We need to whisper," I said. "Frank, can you be lookout?"

Frank climbed up to the next branch, where there was a gap in the canopy. Molly shifted impatiently.

"Come on, Anna. Spit it out. It can't be that important."

Anger flared inside me.

"It's about as important as anything could be. I wouldn't tell you unless it was important."

She frowned. "What is it then?"

My stomach felt like a pit of snakes. I couldn't believe this was happening.

"He's German," I whispered.

"What?" Molly looked blank.

"That man. He's not a British soldier. Everything he told us was a lie."

"What are you talking about?"

"When I went back in the barn, I heard him swear in German. He didn't know I was there. He's German."

For a minute, she just stared at me. Then she

153

whispered, "So you mean ... he's a spy? A German spy?"

"Oh, my goodness," said Frank, his eyes huge. "A German spy in our barn. Oh, my goodness. We need to tell the warden." He climbed down from his lookout branch and tugged at Molly's arm. "Quick, let's go."

Molly shook her arm free. "Get off, Frank." She turned to me. "Are you really sure he's German? He doesn't sound a bit foreign."

"Perhaps he's lived in England for a long time. But he's definitely German. He started muttering to himself, and it sounded German, but I thought I must be imagining it. But then he dropped something and swore, and it was definitely German."

"He must have come down in a parachute," said Frank. "That's probably how he sprained his ankle, not from tripping in a ditch at all. And how he got the blood and scratches on his face. He probably landed in brambles." His eyes shone with excitement. "I can't believe there's a real German spy in our barn."

"His ankle," I said in relief. "I'd forgotten the sprained ankle. So at least he can't get away at the moment. Let's go and report him, quick."

Molly shrieked. She clapped her hands to her mouth. Her eyes were huge and panicked.

"What is it?" I asked. "What's wrong?"

"Oh no, oh no, oh no!" wailed Molly.

"What?" I said. "What is it?"

"If he's a German spy," whispered Molly, her voice muffled through her palms, "then we've just given top-secret information straight to the enemy."

I frowned, replaying the conversation in my head. "No, we haven't. We didn't tell him anything. We just asked him questions."

"*You* didn't tell him anything. But before you came in..." She groaned, and covered her face with her hands again.

Frank gasped. "Oh, no! It was me. It's all my fault. Oh, no!"

"What? What did you say?"

Molly shook her head. "I'm not saying it again. We should never have said it the first time. Nobody should ever have said it."

Anger rose inside me again. "Molly, you have to tell me. This isn't a game."

Molly shuddered. I tried to contain my irritation.

"Take a deep breath and tell me."

Her deep breath was more like a gasp. She glanced at Frank, whose eyes were shiny with tears.

"Frank heard Dad tell Mum," Molly whispered. "Dad heard it from Mr Robins – you know, the butler at the big house. The one you thought was Lord Hurstwood. Dad told Mum secretly in the garden, but Frank was in the Anderson and he overheard. And then he told me in the barn."

"So what's the secret? It can't be that bad."

Tears welled up in Molly's eyes.

"Winston Churchill is coming here on Thursday."

I stared at her.

"Winston Churchill? The Prime Minister?"

Molly burst into tears.

"Stop it," I hissed. "This is important. Stop crying and tell me exactly what you said."

I could tell she was trying to stop, but it took ages before the crying turned into shuddering sobs. Frank was crying too. I had to bite my cheeks to stop myself from shouting at them.

Eventually Molly took a juddery breath and said, "Mr Robins told Dad that he'd been told to expect a very special guest for lunch on Thursday. And then he was asked to find this particular bottle of champagne from the wine cellar and order a particular box of cigars. And he said that type of champagne is Mr Churchill's favourite and those cigars are the kind he always smokes. So he's certain the Prime Minister is coming on Thursday to inspect the troops."

I felt hollow.

"And Frank told you all that in the barn?"

Molly covered her face with her hands and nodded. "We just told a German spy that the British Prime Minister is coming here on Thursday." She started to cry again. "If Winston Churchill's killed, it will be our fault."

Frank's sobs grew even louder. A strange feeling came over me: a feeling of calmness and strength. I had to take control of the situation.

"All right," I said. "Let's not panic. We've seen his ankle. That was one thing he couldn't lie about. It's a bad sprain, and it might even be broken. He won't be able to go anywhere for a while, so even if he did hear what you said, he can't pass on a message. And he might not even have heard, because he said he

156

was asleep, remember?"

Frank's sobbing lessened. He looked at me hopefully.

"But he would say that, wouldn't he?" said Molly. "I'm sure he heard every word we said. We weren't even whispering."

"But he can't tell anyone else. He's stuck in the barn. And just to make sure, two of us can keep watch at the door while the other one runs for the warden or the policeman."

"He might have a wireless transmitter to send Morse code messages back to Germany," said Frank. "Spies all carry Morse code transmitters. He might have sent a message already."

I looked at him in horror. Of course.

"How big is a wireless transmitter?" I asked. "He only had that rucksack."

"He might have been hiding it," said Frank. "He'd have to hide it, wouldn't he?"

"Right. We've got no time to lose. One of us must go for the warden straightaway, while the other two take him the water and keep him in conversation. We have to make sure he's arrested before he can cause any damage."

"If he's already sent a message," said Molly, "then he's already caused damage."

Panic rose inside me, but I tried not to show it. "The police will make him tell them if he's sent any messages, and then they'll sort it out. They won't let Winston Churchill come here if there's any danger." I stood up. "Come on. Let's go. We mustn't waste any more time."

I started to climb down the ladder, but Molly gasped and gripped my arm. She was deathly white.

"No! We can't tell anyone."

"What are you talking about?" said Frank. "Of course we've got to—"

"Don't you see?" hissed Molly. "If we get him arrested, they'll make him tell them what he knows, and then they'll find out that Mr Robins told Dad about Mr Churchill coming, and Dad told Mum, which was giving away a national secret, and Mr Robins and Dad will get arrested."

Frank turned pale. "They wouldn't arrest Dad, would they?"

"Of course they would. Not just arrest him either. You know what the sentence is for passing on state secrets?"

A tight ball of anger was forming in the pit of my stomach.

"Molly, don't be stupid. We have to report this."

"No, we don't!" Molly was hysterical now. "Don't you understand? People who pass on state secrets get the death sentence. Dad could be hanged!"

Frank burst into tears again.

"Stop crying, Frank," Molly snapped. "That isn't going to happen. Because we're not going to tell anyone. Are we, Anna?" She gave me a fierce look.

I was so furious I was actually trembling. "So you want to keep a Nazi spy in the barn, and take him food and water, knowing he knows the Prime Minister's coming here on Thursday? Are you mad as well as stupid?"

"We just have to stop him passing on information to Germany," said Molly. "If we make sure he doesn't do that, then we're not doing any harm, are we?"

"You really are mad, aren't you? Well, I'm going to report him if you won't."

I climbed down the ladder before she could grab me again. I started to run up the field, but Molly was a faster runner than me and she caught up with me and grabbed the back of my shirt before I was halfway to the gate.

I whirled round to face her.

"You accuse me of being a Nazi!" I hissed. "It's you who's the Nazi! You want to leave him in the barn, sending messages to Germany so Hitler can blow up the Prime Minister and all those soldiers! And what happens if Churchill gets killed? Then Britain has no leader and Hitler wins the war. And do you know what that means? No, of course you don't. You haven't a clue. But I know. I know what it's like to live under Hitler. And if you don't report this man, then you'll very soon know what it's like too. So I'm going to report him right now and you'd better not try to stop me."

I turned to run. But Frank grabbed my hand in both of his. His eyes were huge in his tear-streaked face.

"Please, Anna," he sobbed. "Please don't get Daddy hanged. Please, please don't let Daddy die."

"Don't be stupid," I said. "Of course he won't—"

Then, looking at the desperate terror in Frank's

face, I stopped.

I had been going to say, of course Uncle Bert won't be hanged. But now it hit me for the first time that this wasn't actually true.

One of the first things Churchill had done when he became Prime Minister was to pass the Treachery Act. Molly was right. The sentence for passing on a state secret was death. Their father might actually be hanged.

Good, kind, gentle Uncle Bert, hanged for treason? How could I let that happen?

But how could I not report a Nazi spy?

"Look," said Molly. "The most important thing – the only important thing at the moment – is to make sure he can't pass on any messages."

"And what if he's already done that?"

She was silent for a while. Then she said, "All right. Here's what we're going to do. We'll take him some water, like we said we would. And while we're there, we'll find out if he has a wireless set. If he does, we'll have to report him."

Frank gasped. "No! We can't!"

"We have to," she said. "We don't have to say anything about Dad. Maybe they won't find out. But Anna's right. We can't just let a German spy live in the barn, sending messages back to Hitler. We can't put the whole country at risk."

CHAPTER THIRTY

"Hide Your Maps"
If the Invader Comes

Frank and I waited in the farmyard while Molly went indoors to get the water. She took forever. I thought I'd explode with frustration.

"What's she doing in there?" I muttered to Frank, as I paced up and down by the garden wall. "Doesn't she realise it's urgent? He could have sent hundreds of messages by now. There might be bomber planes on their way already."

Frank gave a strangled whimper. Immediately I felt bad. I squeezed his hand.

"Don't worry, Frank. There won't really be planes coming yet. Even Hitler isn't that fast."

I tried to speak lightly, but I was terrified. There was no time to spare.

Eventually Molly reappeared with a jug of water and a glass.

"What took you so long?" I said.

Molly frowned. "What do you mean? I was only gone a couple of minutes."

"Come on," I said, hurrying towards the barn.

"Remember, Frank," said Molly, "we have to act as though we completely believe his story. Just be very

161

sympathetic, but if he asks you for any information, you absolutely mustn't give it to him."

"But how can I not give it to him without making him suspicious?" asked Frank.

"Just pretend to be very, very stupid," said Molly. "Whatever he asks you, tell him you don't know."

As we approached the half-open door of the barn, we all fell silent. Suddenly I had an idea. I signalled for the other two to stop.

"I'm going to listen at the door for a minute," I whispered, "in case he's talking to himself in German again. I'll signal for you."

I tiptoed to the doorway and slipped inside.

Sure enough, the man was muttering under his breath. I had to strain to hear his mumbling. It took a while to tune out the sounds of the farmyard and make out any individual words. They were pretty much all swear words.

Hearing him speak German churned up my insides. The last time I'd heard German had been on the journey to England.

He seemed to be concentrating intently on something.

"*Mist ... ach, mein Gott ... ist kaputt...*"

Kaputt.

Broken.

The relief was dizzying. I felt like a balloon that had been tethered to the ground by a lead weight. Now the weight had been cut and I was floating up into the air. I tiptoed out and beckoned the others further away.

"It's broken," I whispered, when we were at a safe distance.

"His wireless?" asked Molly, her face tense with anxiety.

"Yes. I heard him swearing, and then he said, '*Ist kaputt*.' That means 'It's broken' in German."

"Are you sure it was the wireless that was broken though? Did you see it?"

The balloon burst.

"No," I said flatly. "I didn't see it."

"It must have been his wireless," said Frank. "What else would be broken?"

"All sorts of things," said Molly. "He might have masses of other spy equipment in that rucksack. Or it could be something else, nothing to do with his spy equipment."

"Like his shoelace," said Frank unhelpfully.

"I tell you what," said Molly. "We'll walk up to the barn quietly, so he doesn't hear us coming. Then we'll go in together and climb the ladder really quickly. Whatever's broken, he'll have to put it away fast, and he probably won't have time to hide it very well. One of us can keep him talking – I'll do that – while you look around for a wireless set, Anna. And if we find it, we need to disable it."

"How?" asked Frank.

"I don't know," said Molly. "We'll just have to think of something."

We crept across the yard, our plimsolls soundless on the concrete. At the barn door, Molly turned to Frank.

"Act normal," she mouthed. "Remember, we think he's an English soldier who wants to see his sick mother."

She sauntered into the barn.

Something slid across the loft floor. A wireless set? There was no way of knowing. Hay rustled. Was he hiding something?

Molly climbed the ladder quickly. I went next. As my eyes drew level with the loft floor, I saw the man withdraw his hand from a pile of loose hay to the right of him. Was that where he had hidden his radio? Had Molly noticed it too?

Clover was snuggled by his side, purring. That cat had no loyalty.

"Hello, Mr Smith," said Molly. "Frank's got your water."

I reached down and took the jug and glass from Frank. He started to climb up as I poured a glass of water for the man and handed it to him.

"Thank you," he said. "You are very kind."

He drained the glass in one gulp and held it out to me. I refilled it and set the half-empty jug beside him.

It was horrible, being nice to him, knowing who he really was and what he might be planning to do. I felt like a traitor for simply giving him a glass of water. No. I *was* a traitor for giving him a glass of water.

He stroked Clover. I felt such a surge of hatred that I had to look at the floor in case he could read my feelings.

"How's your ankle?" asked Molly.

He pulled a pained face. "Bad. I have tried, but I cannot walk on it at all."

That was good news. Maybe it was broken. We just had to make sure his wireless was properly broken too.

"We'll bring you some food later," said Molly. "We can't get it at the moment because Mum's cooking tea, but I can sneak into the larder later and get you some leftovers. Do you like meat pie?"

While Molly kept him in conversation about food and the problems of rationing, I scrutinised the heap of loose hay. It was the obvious place to hide a wireless set.

On his left-hand side lay his rucksack. It was open at the top. It would be good to get a look in there too.

"I wonder if you could find me a map?" he said to Molly. "I need to get to my mother's village, you see. It is near Whitstable. Are we close to Whitstable? We were not told the place where we were billeted, you see, and it is so hard to tell where one is, with no signposts."

I glanced at Molly. Did the man really not know where he was? It was quite possible, if he had parachuted down from a plane at night.

"We don't have any maps, I'm afraid," said Molly. "I'm not sure how far we are from Whitstable."

I had a sudden thought. If the man really didn't know where he was, then we could tell him he was somewhere else. Not somewhere too far away, obviously, but far enough to mislead him.

I grabbed Frank's hand and squeezed it, hoping he would understand the squeeze as a code to keep quiet. I wished I could make eye contact with Molly, but that would be impossible without the man noticing.

"The nearest town is Cranbrook," I said, squeezing Frank's hand harder. Cranbrook was actually about twenty miles away.

Molly flicked a quick glance at me. Then she started to speak, and my stomach clenched in terror. *Please don't ruin it*, I prayed. If we blew this chance to mislead him, we'd never have another opportunity.

"This village is called Muddle Green," she said.

She had understood! Muddle Green was the village where Molly and Frank's grandparents lived. It was quite close to Cranbrook, but several miles away from Ashcombe.

"Muddle Green," repeated the man thoughtfully. "Near Cranbrook."

"And this estate where we live," said Molly, "and where you were billeted, is called Peasmarsh."

"Peasmarsh," repeated the man. I wondered where Molly had got that name from.

"My dad works on the estate," said Molly. "He's a carpenter."

"A carpenter?" said the man. "That is a very interesting job, no?"

He sounded more relaxed than he had done before. My mind went back to the wireless set. The man now thought he had valuable information as to the whereabouts of a huge contingent of British troops. Surely the first thing he would do when he was on his own again would be to try to fix his wireless set and send a message to Germany. And what if the Germans decided to bomb Muddle Green?

Molly was chattering on about her dad's work on the estate. "He's just made new doors for all the pigsties. Pigs are the worst, he says. You wouldn't believe how they bash their doors about. He's always mending them. They love to perch with their trotters up on the tops of the doors and look out, you see. They're very curious animals, pigs. But they weigh a ton, and sooner or later the doors break under the strain."

"I have one more favour to ask," said the man. "I must write a letter to my mother. I wrote in my last letter that I would be with her today, and when I don't arrive, she will worry. If I write to her today, would you be able to post the letter?"

"Of course," said Molly. "We'll be passing the post box in the morning, when we go to the shop for your food."

"Thank you," he said.

He drained his water glass again, and suddenly I had an idea.

"More?" I said.

I reached for the jug. As I picked it up, I purposely tripped over his outstretched leg and collapsed on to the floor, spilling the water into the pile of hay.

Surely that amount of water would destroy a wireless set?

The man let out a howl of fury. He grabbed a handful of dry hay and dropped it on top of the wet stuff, scrabbling around underneath and pulling the soggy hay out. He was clearly trying to wipe up the mess without exposing whatever was underneath it. But as I watched him, he accidentally pushed the hay aside, and I saw.

As he quickly swept hay over the exposed surface, I leaned over to the other side of him and picked up his glass, so he wouldn't suspect that I'd seen anything.

And also to hide my bitter disappointment. Because what I had seen was not a wet and ruined wireless transmitter.

There *was* a wireless transmitter underneath that pile of hay, I had no doubt. But even if I'd poured ten jugs of water on it, it wouldn't have been destroyed. Because what I had seen was the smooth brown lid of a leather case.

"I'm so sorry," I said. "I'm terribly clumsy. I hope I didn't spill anything on you."

The man stiffened. He stared at me, his eyes narrowed.

"Sorry. I didn't hear what you said. Could you repeat it, please?"

My heart thumped. I forced myself to smile, desperately hoping he couldn't sense my fear.

"I'm very sorry. I hope I didn't spill anything on you."

Still staring at me, the man gave a fake smile.

"Don't worry," he said. "All is well."

"I'll fetch more water." I had to get away from him.

"No, no." Then he said, obviously trying to sound as though he was simply making a casual remark, "Your accent is interesting. You do not sound like your brother and sister."

"Oh, Anna's not our sister," said Molly breezily. "She's an evacuee. There's loads of evacuees in the village."

The man raised his eyebrows. "An evacuee? That is very interesting. What part of England do you come from?"

"London," said Molly.

"London?" said the man. "I see."

It was no use pretending. He could clearly tell.

"I did come from London," I said, "but that was my aunt's home. I'm actually from Germany."

There was a terrible pause. It felt as though the world had stopped. We all looked at the man, as he looked at me.

Then, as if he had just remembered that he was supposed to be an ordinary British soldier, he said, "From Germany. How interesting."

There was another awkward silence. Frank spoke first.

"Shall I go and get you some more water? It's no trouble, honestly."

"No, no," said the man. "I am very tired. I think I shall sleep now."

"Sorry about Anna spilling the water," said Molly. "I hope your ankle feels better soon. We'll bring you some food later."

We climbed down the ladder and walked back across the yard and down to the tree house. We climbed into it and parted the leaves to scan the horizon in all directions.

Once we were sure we were alone, Frank was the first to speak.

"He's scary. I don't like him."

He was scary. And now he knew I was German. I bet he'd guessed I was Jewish, too. What might he try to do to me now?

But I didn't say any of that. I didn't want to make Frank any more frightened than he was already. Instead, I said, "His wireless transmitter is in a case. So the water didn't destroy it."

"Oh!" said Frank, wide-eyed. "Did you spill it on purpose?"

Molly rolled her eyes. Then she said, "I saw something, too. Next to his transmitter."

"What?" asked Frank.

"He covered it up again with hay, and he didn't realise I'd seen it," Molly said. "He's got a gun."

CHAPTER THIRTY-ONE

"Keep Watch"
If the Invader Comes

Fear shuddered through me like an electric shock. I saw storm troopers bursting into my bedroom, waving their rifles. I saw the SS man pointing his gun at Ezra's basket.

"We have to tell someone," I said. My voice was small and strained.

"We can't," said Molly. "They'd arrest him and make him tell them everything he knows, and then Dad would be arrested."

"He's got a gun, Molly," I said. "What if he breaks into the house tonight and kills us all?"

Frank made a strangled sobbing sound. Molly shot me a fierce look.

"Don't be stupid. Why would he do that? He's a spy, not a murderer. He's here to send messages back to Germany, not kill people. Anyway, he needs us to bring him food and water. And he can't even walk at the moment. So I don't know why you're saying ridiculous things like that, just to frighten Frank."

"It's not to frighten Frank," I said. My voice came out strangely.

The garden gate squeaked open and Aunty Rose's

voice called, "Molly! Frank! Anna! Are you out here?"

Molly leaned over the edge of the platform, parted the leaves and called, "We're in the tree house."

"Supper's nearly ready. Come down and wash your hands."

"Coming," said Molly.

We waited as the footsteps receded. When we heard the back door shut again, Molly turned to me and said, "Listen. He can't do any harm at the moment, can he? His wireless is broken, his ankle is most likely broken, and he'll probably spend all night sleeping."

"But what if he mends his wireless? We know he was trying to mend it before. He told us to go away so he could sleep, didn't he? I bet he's busy mending it right now."

"It might be completely broken," said Molly. "He might not be able to mend it at all."

"But he might. We don't know."

"Maybe that's why he asked us to post a letter," said Frank. "If he can't get his wireless working, he'll need to write to people instead."

I looked at Frank with new respect. "Of course! We know he's not really writing to his mother."

"So he's writing to his spymasters back in Germany," said Molly, "and feeding them information. Or he's part of a spy ring in this country, and they need to communicate with each other to plan their attacks."

Frank's eyes sparkled. "I bet it will be in code! We can steam it open and crack the code!"

172

"Great sort of code it will be if a seven-year-old can crack it," said Molly.

"So we need to pass it on to somebody," I said. "You must see that, Molly. We can't keep this to ourselves. That letter will be passing on secret information, and the government needs to know about it."

"But he doesn't actually know any secret information, does he?" said Molly. "We fooled him, didn't we? He doesn't actually know where Mr Churchill will be because we gave him the wrong information. So even if he does send a message, they won't attack here."

Frank gasped. "No, they'll attack Muddle Green. They'll attack Granny and Grandad."

Molly turned pale. Then she said, "They won't be able to find it. There's no signposts."

"They probably have maps," I said. "Or they'll be disguised as British soldiers, like he is, and they'll trick somebody into giving them directions."

"But even if they do get there, they'll see there aren't any soldiers there and they'll know they're in the wrong place."

"So then they'll get really angry and come here and kill us because we lied to them," said Frank.

"Or the Luftwaffe might bomb Muddle Green from the air," I said.

Frank's eyes filled with tears. "This is bad. It's really bad. We should tell someone."

"We have to think of something," said Molly. "We have to think of a way to get him caught without

Dad getting into trouble."

"We could ask him not to tell about Dad," said Frank.

Molly gave him a withering look. "He's a Nazi, Frank. I don't think they care about being kind to people."

"No," I said. "They don't. We have to tell the police. And if you don't, I shall."

Molly and I stared at each other for a moment. Then she said, "All right. This is what we'll do. We'll take turns to watch him. We'll hide in the barn. If we creep in through that gap in the wall under the loft where the plank's missing, he won't see us coming or going. We'll sit right underneath the loft and hear every move he makes. And if he does get his wireless mended and sends a message, we'll tell the police immediately, all right? But if he doesn't, everybody's safe. And then tomorrow we'll find a way to properly destroy his wireless so he can't do any more damage."

"And after that?" I said. "What about when his ankle gets better and he tries to get away?"

"I don't know yet. But it gives us a bit more time to think of something."

The back gate opened again. "Molly!" called Aunty Rose. "Come in for tea right now, all of you!"

"Coming!" yelled Molly. She stood up and started to climb down the rope ladder. "Right," she whispered. "Who's doing the first shift?"

CHAPTER THIRTY-TWO

"Use Your Common Sense"

If the Invader Comes

Everything had to be decided in the short walk from the tree house to the cottage. We settled on two hours each. I volunteered to take the first shift. If I missed supper, it would arouse less suspicion. It was unheard of for Molly or Frank to miss a meal.

Molly and I both thought Frank was too young to sit in the dark barn all alone, but he wouldn't hear of missing out.

"All right," whispered Molly. We were almost at the house by now. "We haven't got time to argue. But you'll just do one hour, not two. You do the second shift. You'll have to pretend to go to bed as usual, and then creep outside. We'll talk more about it after supper. Then I'll do the third shift. I'll take him some food and go in by the door. Taking him food will give me the chance to see what he's up to. And when I've taken up his food, I'll go out of the big door, so he thinks I've left, and creep in again through the gap in the wall. I'll wake Anna at ten, and the two of us will take turns during the night. Don't argue, Frank," she said, as he started to interrupt. "You're lucky you're even allowed to do one shift. I'd much rather you didn't."

As the others washed their hands at the sink in the scullery, I said, "Aunty Rose, I'm feeling a bit sick. Would it be all right if I went and lay down for a while?"

Aunty Rose frowned in concern. "I hope you're not coming down with something." She laid her hand on my forehead. "You don't feel hot."

"Maybe it was something she ate," suggested Molly, coming in from the scullery. "She scoffed lots of raspberries in the tree house."

I shot her a look. It was a bit much, Molly accusing *me* of greed.

"Some of them weren't very ripe," Molly continued. "That's probably why she's got a tummy ache."

Aunty Rose shook her head and tutted. "Well, go and lie down, Anna. You two come and have your supper."

I had to admit that a stomach ache from eating unripe raspberries was a good idea. Faking actual illness might lead to all sorts of complications, whereas this could be over in a couple of hours, just as I finished my shift in the barn.

The only problem would be if Aunty Rose came upstairs to check on me. I knew Molly would do all she could to prevent that, but I wished we'd had a chance to discuss it. It would have been one less thing to worry about.

I arranged my pillow lengthways in the bed, with the covers on top of it. Then I closed the curtains.

With any luck, if Aunty Rose did come to check, she would see the shape in the bed and leave the room without investigating any further.

I started to tiptoe downstairs, desperately hoping the boards wouldn't creak. Luckily there was plenty of noise in the kitchen.

"Give your dad some more potatoes, Molly," Aunty Rose was saying. "He's worn out after digging those defence trenches."

"Where are the trenches?" asked Frank. "Can we play in them?"

"Up under the wood," said Uncle Bert. "Just above Neaves Lane."

"Oh, that reminds me," said Aunty Rose. "I saw Mrs Chantrey today. She's going up to Scotland to stay with her daughter. She says she can't bear the sound of the planes every night and she's too old to be spending the night in shelters. They're not getting any air raids up where her daughter lives, she says."

"Lucky them," said Uncle Bert.

"She's going to give me the keys to her cottage," said Aunty Rose. "She's got tenants moving in, but not for a couple of weeks, so I said I'd water her plants and send on her post in the meantime."

Uncle Bert tutted. "Haven't you got enough to do, with all the WVS and WI things you're taking on? This house is like a jam factory at the moment. I haven't had a decent meal in weeks."

The children laughed. Uncle Bert loved to grumble, but he didn't mean any of it.

"Weren't you in the Dog and Duck with Jack

Hawkins last night?" said Aunty Rose. "Mrs Chantrey told me she found him asleep in the ditch outside her house this morning, with his bicycle on top of him."

Frank went off into peals of laughter. "Asleep in the ditch! Why was he asleep in the ditch?"

Uncle Bert chuckled. "He did get a bit merry, but I didn't know he was that far gone."

"Didn't turn up for milking, apparently. Mr Parris had to send William out to find him. Jack told Mrs Chantrey it was the best night's sleep he'd had in months."

As they laughed and chatted, I tiptoed down the last few stairs and into the porch. I inched the front door open and slipped outside.

The farmyard was bathed in late afternoon golden light. The farm workers were all out haymaking in the fields. The sounds of the army camp drifted across from the Park. A pig grunted in its sty. I made my way across the yard and, holding my breath, inched through the narrow gap in the barn wall.

I stood still and listened.

There was no sound from the loft. Assuming the man hadn't moved, he would be directly above me right now. With a gun by his side.

That was a horrible thought. I tried to put it out of my mind and concentrate instead on deciding where to sit for the next two hours.

There was an upturned bucket a couple of metres away. It wouldn't be the most comfortable seat, but it might be better than the dirt floor.

The loft was completely silent. Maybe he had been telling the truth when he said he was going to sleep. I wished I could hear snoring, so I could be sure. It was even more frightening than I'd expected, sitting in the gloom with an armed Nazi spy on a wooden platform directly above me. My heart thumped and my palms were sweating. I was terrified I would accidentally make a sound and give myself away.

I forced my mind to concentrate on finding a solution to the terrible situation we were in. A solution where Uncle Bert wouldn't get into trouble and the man wouldn't be able to give away his secrets.

Suddenly my eyes opened wide and my heart started racing.

There was a solution.

But did I have the courage to do what it would take?

It took a while to slow down my racing mind and start to think properly. But when I did, I realised that what I'd thought was a hideous mess was actually an incredible opportunity. Finally I had the chance to really help the war effort. And if I didn't take this chance then I would be betraying everybody I loved.

A huge snort came from the loft. I jumped in shock, biting my tongue with the effort of stifling a shriek. The snort was followed by a grunt and a noisy rustling. Clearly the man had been asleep, and clearly he was now waking up.

My heart was thumping. What if he climbed down

and found me?

I remembered his swollen ankle. But what if he was really determined to get away? After all, he had managed to climb up using only one leg.

Various disgusting nasal noises came from the loft.

The church clock struck seven. Frank would be here any minute. I didn't like the thought of leaving him alone with the man, especially now he was awake.

A shadow fell across the barn floor. My stomach turned over. But it was only Frank, climbing through the gap. Through a series of complicated hand signals, I managed to communicate that he should leave the barn and that I would come out too because I wanted to talk to him.

We tiptoed across the yard and into the cowshed.

"He's just woken up," I whispered. "I'll stay with you. You shouldn't be alone with him."

Frank shook his head. "You have to go back. Mum's going to come to your room to see how you're feeling. She was going to go in when she came to say goodnight to me, but I told her I'd just gone in and you were asleep. But she'll come and check on you soon, so you have to be there."

"What about Molly? She could come out."

"Mum's got her scrubbing potatoes and washing the eggs. I'll be fine, honest. I'm not scared or anything. I want to do it."

I looked at him. He seemed very determined.

"All right. But if you're scared by anything he says or does, or if he mends the machine and starts talking or using code or anything, you must come and get me straightaway, all right?"

"I will. Was he trying to fix the transmitter while you were there?"

"No. He only woke up a few minutes ago. That's why I think he might start working on it now."

"I wonder if he's got a torch," said Frank.

That was a very good question. If he didn't have a torch, he wouldn't be able to work on his machine once it got dark.

"Let's hope he doesn't."

"You'd better go and get into bed," said Frank.

"Good luck. Come and tell me about it when you get back."

Molly would take over at eight o'clock. Then I would take over from Molly at ten. And I would bring a loaded shotgun with me.

CHAPTER THIRTY-THREE

"Be Ready to Help the Military In Any Way"

If the Invader Comes

"He asked me to bring him a battery for his torch," whispered Molly. "Can you believe the cheek of it? Obviously I told him we didn't have any spares. And that's not even a lie. They haven't had them in the shop for weeks. Then he asked if he could borrow mine! I said Mum and Dad would go mad if the torch was missing, so I couldn't risk it."

She had come to wake me at five past ten. Not that I had been asleep. You don't fall asleep when you're planning to kill a man in three hours' time.

Those three hours had been the longest of my life. I don't know how I endured them. I tried to block out all thoughts by filling my head with other things: poems we'd learned in school; times tables; capital cities; anything to keep the terror away.

Molly was sitting on the edge of my bed, whispering excitedly in the darkness. I barely heard a word she said. An ice-cold fog of dread enveloped me.

What would happen to me after I'd killed him?

I wouldn't be hanged, would I? Surely they didn't hang children in England? Besides, I was killing a Nazi. The English wouldn't hang a person who killed a Nazi. Would they?

"Anna? Are you listening?"

"No, I... What did you say?"

"Why are your teeth chattering? It's not cold." She felt my forehead. "You're freezing. Are you sick?"

I shook my head. "I'm fine."

"Well, put your jumper on. You might be cold sitting in the barn for two hours."

"I'm fine, honestly." I tried to clamp my jaws together to stop my teeth chattering. It didn't work.

"I was saying I think he's trying to get his transmitter working. I heard him fiddling with something after he thought I'd left the barn. Then his torch battery ran out, thank goodness, and he cursed and swore like anything. Well, it was in German, but it definitely sounded like swearing. Then he went quiet, so I think he's gone back to sleep."

I stood up. "I must go."

"Good luck. See you in two hours."

I felt so sick that I had to hold on to the doorframe to steady myself. When *would* Molly see me next? After I'd been arrested for murder?

Gripping the doorframe, I forced myself to take deep breaths.

"Are you sure you're all right?" Molly sounded worried. "Do you want me to do the shift instead?"

I shook my head. "I'm fine," I said again. Then I left the room and tiptoed downstairs, leaning on the banister to let it take as much of my weight as possible so the bare boards didn't creak beneath my feet.

In the dark kitchen, I felt my way to the drawer where Aunty Rose kept the matches. I struck one, holding my breath in fear that the sound would wake somebody.

All was silent.

I lit the candle that stood in an enamel saucer on the cupboard. In the shadowy light, I gingerly placed a chair in front of the dresser. Standing on the chair, I swept my hand along the top of the dresser until it touched a key. Then I stepped off the chair and unlocked the tall narrow cupboard where Uncle Bert kept his gun, loaded and ready to shoot invading Germans. I clasped the cold metal barrel, lifted the gun out and closed the cupboard door.

I had never touched a gun before. It was horrible.

Creak.

It came from upstairs. I stood rigid, clutching the gun. My heart thumped so hard that it felt as though it might burst through my ribcage.

Silence. It must have been someone turning over in their sleep.

I locked the cupboard and replaced the key. Then I opened the back door.

It was brighter outside than I'd expected. The night was cloudless and the sky was full of stars. I felt horribly exposed as I inched my way down the front path and out of the gate.

I would creep into the barn and climb the loft steps as silently as I could. I had to shoot him before he woke up and shot me.

Molly had said it was pitch black in the barn.

Once I was inside, I would have to wait until my eyes adjusted to the dark.

Distant voices from the army camp drifted across the fields.

I knew soldiers patrolled the Park perimeter at night. What would I do when the gunshot shattered the silence and the soldiers came running?

Panic rose inside me.

No. I mustn't think about that. I must just do what I had to do.

I had no idea how to fire a gun. I should at least practise aiming it.

I lifted it to shoulder height and moved my finger towards the trigger.

"Stop right there! Drop your weapon and put your hands in the air."

I jumped and shrieked. The shotgun clattered to the ground.

"Put your hands in the air!"

From the shadows between the buildings strode a soldier, pointing a gun at me. The world spun. My legs dissolved. The ground tilted beneath me. The soldier grabbed my arm.

"What the blazes? You're just a kid. What the hell are you up to?"

My teeth chattered. I was freezing cold.

Keeping his eyes fixed on mine, the soldier picked up my rifle.

"Put your hands behind your back," he ordered in a low voice.

"No! Don't tie me up. Please!"

"Put your hands behind your back."

I put my hands behind my back, clasping them together as tightly as I could to stop them shaking.

"You don't sound English," he said. "Where are you from?"

My stomach clenched. In a flash, I saw how this would look to the soldier. A German with a gun, out in the middle of the night, walking towards an army base. I felt my insides dissolving.

"I'm a refugee."

"What nationality?"

I felt so sick I could hardly speak. "I'm German," I whispered. "But I'm not a Nazi. I'm a Jewish refugee. I hate Hitler. I hate him more than anybody."

With his free hand, the soldier took my wrists in a firm grip and started to lead me out of the farmyard.

"Where are you taking me?" My voice was small and shaky.

"To my commanding officer," he said. "You're under arrest."

CHAPTER THIRTY-FOUR

"Go Quickly to the Nearest Authority and Give Him the Facts"
If the Invader Comes

I stumbled beside the soldier as he marched me along the lane, up the tree-lined avenue and right to the foot of the broad stone steps that led to the gigantic carved front doors of Ashcombe House. We stopped in front of another soldier with a gun, standing at the foot of the steps.

"Permission to see Colonel Ferguson," said the soldier with me. "I have a suspect for interrogation."

Interrogation?

Images flashed through my mind. Storm troopers in jackboots, kicking old men in the street. Rifle butts jammed into faces. Windows smashed, doors kicked in. My father returning from Buchenwald, covered in cuts and bruises.

My legs buckled under me. The soldier jerked me upright. He led me along a path that ran around the side of the house to another entrance. Another armed soldier stood on guard in front of the door.

"Private Willis to see Colonel Ferguson," said the soldier, still gripping my wrists. "Suspect for interrogation."

The guard let us into the building. In the corridor

stood another soldier. Private Willis explained that he was bringing me to Colonel Ferguson. The soldier led us up a flight of stairs and along corridors until we came to a large landing. Several grand, elaborately carved doors led off the landing. The soldier knocked on one of these.

"Come in," said a voice from inside the room.

The soldier stepped inside.

"Private Willis requesting to see you, sir," he said. "He has somebody with him. Says it's a suspect for interrogation, sir... Yes, sir."

He stepped back out and gestured for Private Willis to go in. Still clasping my wrists, Private Willis led me into the room.

A broad-shouldered man sat frowning from a leather armchair by the fireplace of the very grand drawing room, his long legs stretched out in front of him. Presumably this was Colonel Ferguson, although he didn't look at all as I'd imagined an interrogating officer would look. He wore a tweed jacket and corduroy trousers, with tweed slippers on his feet. He held a lit cigarette in one hand and there was a book on his lap. One finger was between the pages of his book, marking his place. The book was called *Right Ho, Jeeves*.

He glanced at Private Willis and then turned his gaze on me. His frown deepened. He glared at the soldier.

"What the blazes do you think you're playing at, Willis? Is this meant to be some kind of joke?"

"No, sir," said Private Willis. "I was on perimeter

duty, sir, when I saw this girl crossing the farmyard. She was carrying this shotgun, sir. And she's German, sir."

Colonel Ferguson looked intently at me. Then he rose from the armchair, put his book down on a side table and strode to the other end of the room, where a big desk made of polished wood sat on a patterned rug. On the desk was a telephone, a box of notepaper, a pen, an inkstand and a blotting pad.

The colonel sat down in the chair behind the desk and indicated for me and Private Willis to stand on the other side of it.

"You can let go of her now, Willis. I don't think she's going to make a run for it."

Private Willis let go of my wrists.

"So," said the colonel, "explain yourself, Willis."

When he had heard the soldier's account, Colonel Ferguson turned to me.

"What is your name?"

"Anna Schlesinger."

"And would you mind telling me, Anna Schlesinger, what exactly you were planning to do with that gun?"

I pictured Uncle Bert going out at night with the shotgun.

"I was going to shoot rabbits," I said. "To make a stew."

The colonel raised his eyebrows and gave me a penetrating look. I shifted my gaze to the rug.

"Why don't you tell me the truth?" he said.

I wished I could tell him the truth. I wished I could

leave this horrible situation for the army to sort out. They would arrest the man immediately and I wouldn't have to have anything more to do with him. But I couldn't risk Uncle Bert being arrested.

The colonel leaned back in his seat. "I can assure you, Miss Schlesinger, that we will find out the truth sooner or later. You'll make it easier for everybody if you tell me yourself and don't waste any more of my time."

I risked a glance at him. Was he threatening me? I didn't believe he would hurt me, but there was a war on, and I was a German who had just been caught sneaking out at night with a loaded gun on an estate full of soldiers.

So I would have to tell him some of the truth.

"I was going to shoot a man," I said.

The colonel's eyes opened very wide.

Private Willis exclaimed in triumph. "I knew it! An enemy agent! There's a network of them, sir. They're everywhere. And they're using kids, little kids, to deceive us all. Can you believe it, sir? Coming over here to kill our troops in their beds. Little kids."

"I'm not a Nazi," I said. "I'm a refugee." I turned to the colonel. "I'm Jewish, sir. I came to England last year on a Kindertransport. I hate the Nazis. They put my father in a concentration camp. They smashed up our apartment. I would never, ever do anything to help them. You have to believe me, sir. Please believe me."

An image came into my head of my parents and

all the awful things that might be happening to them; things I tried so hard not to think about. Tears prickled in the corners of my eyes. I bit my cheeks to stop them coming.

"I'll handle this, Private Willis," said the colonel. He turned back to me. "Explain to me, if you please, exactly who you were planning to shoot and why."

I took a deep breath. I would have to start at the beginning.

Had it really only been this afternoon that we'd found the man? It felt as though it had been going on for months.

"This afternoon," I said, "I was in the barn at Ashcombe Farm, looking for my cat, and a man called to us from the loft and said he had her."

"Us?" said the colonel.

"I was with the children from my foster family. Molly and Frank. We climbed up to the loft and there was a man sitting there, in British battledress. We asked him what he was doing and he said he'd run away from his regiment to visit his sick mother for a few days, but he'd hurt his ankle, so he was resting in the barn until he could walk again. He showed us his ankle, and it was really swollen and bruised, so he wasn't lying about that. He asked us to bring him food and drink. Frank asked his name, and he said he was called Peter Smith."

I paused. The colonel had taken a piece of paper from the box and was writing something down.

"Go on," he said.

"We left the barn, but the cat ran back in, so I

went in after her. I was very quiet and I don't think he knew I was there. I heard something fall over, and then I heard him swear."

My insides turned over at the memory of it.

"In German."

Private Willis gasped. He started to speak but Colonel Ferguson shot him a look.

"What time was this?" the colonel asked.

I thought back. "About four o'clock, I think."

"What did you do after you heard him swear in German?"

I felt sick. How could I possibly answer all his questions without giving everything away?

"I told the others."

"Which others, exactly?"

"Molly and Frank. The children in my host family."

The colonel frowned. "How old are they?"

"Molly's thirteen and Frank's seven."

The colonel's frown deepened. "Did you tell their parents too?"

I felt as though an invisible hand was squeezing my stomach. "No."

"Did you tell another adult? A policeman or a warden, for example?"

I was shaking. "No," I whispered.

Private Willis opened his mouth. Without taking his eyes off my face, the colonel held up a hand to stop him. Private Willis closed his mouth.

The colonel looked at me thoughtfully. After a horribly long silence, he said, "So what did you do once you had told the children?"

I took a deep breath. He wasn't shouting. He didn't seem to be furious. I just needed to stay calm and tell as much of the story as I could without mentioning what Frank had told Molly in the barn.

"Well, we knew he must be a spy, and we thought he might have a Morse code transmitter, so we went back to the loft to take him water and secretly look for a wireless. We wanted to disable it if we could, without him realising what we were doing. We approached the barn very quietly, and I listened at the door before he knew we were there, in case he was saying anything in German. He talks to himself, you see. Muttering under his breath."

The colonel looked very alert.

"And did you hear anything?"

"Yes, sir. I think he was trying to mend his radio set. He was making sounds as though he was annoyed and frustrated, and then I heard him say, '*Ist kaputt.*' That means 'It's broken' in German."

"Go on."

"Well, then we all went into the barn. We were hoping to catch him with the wireless, you see. And as we got up to the loft, I saw him hiding something under some hay, and I was sure it was a wireless, so I pretended to trip up, and I spilled water on it."

The colonel actually looked impressed.

"But when he was wiping up the water I saw a leather lid, and I realised the case was closed so I hadn't damaged the wireless."

"I need you to tell me every detail of the

conversation you had with him at that time," said the colonel. "It's very important that you tell me everything."

"He asked Molly if she had a map. Obviously she said she didn't. He said his mother lived in Whitstable and he wasn't sure how far away that was. He asked the name of this village, and the nearest town, and I realised he didn't know where he was, so we'd be able to trick him."

The colonel narrowed his eyes. "Trick him?"

"Yes, sir. I told him the nearest town was Cranbrook, and this village was called Muddle Green. And Molly said this estate was called Peasmarsh."

The colonel nodded thoughtfully. "I see." He scribbled some notes on the paper. "What else did you tell him? I need to know everything, exactly as you said it, and his replies, exactly as he said them."

I thought back to when Molly had been chatting to the man. I told the colonel everything she'd said about Lord Hurstwood going to Canada, and Uncle Bert's job, and the pigs.

"And then he asked us if we'd post a letter for him."

Colonel Ferguson's eyes widened. He sat up very straight.

"Go on. Tell me exactly what he said about the letter."

I told him everything.

"And Molly said we'd post it in the morning, when we went to the shop for his food. We weren't really going to post it, obviously. He thanked her, and then

I had the idea of spilling the water on his wireless. He was really angry and he told us to leave so he could sleep. So we left, but we decided to guard him all night, in case he got his radio working again and tried to make contact with anyone. If he had done, we would have told the policeman or the warden straightaway. We agreed on that."

I paused, hoping for a sign of approval. There wasn't one. Instead, the colonel said, in a tone I didn't like at all, "How exactly did you plan to guard him?"

I told him how we'd taken it in turns to sit in the barn, and how Molly thought she'd heard him working on his wireless, until his torch battery ran out.

"Molly came to wake me at ten," I finished, "and that's when I went out with the gun and Private Willis caught me."

"And you were planning to kill this man?"

"Yes, sir."

"Permission to speak, sir," said Private Willis.

The colonel gave him an impatient look.

"Go on then, but make it snappy."

The soldier cleared his throat importantly. "I think the girl is spinning you a yarn, sir. She's a German, she admits that herself. I believe she's part of this man's network, and she was smuggling him a loaded weapon. Why else would she fail to inform the appropriate authorities of the presence of a man who on her own admission she knew to be a German spy?"

"I wasn't smuggling him a weapon," I said to the colonel. "I promise I wasn't. Please believe me, sir. I would never supply a weapon to a German."

"I believe you," said the colonel.

Private Willis snorted.

"I believe that you were trying to kill him," said the colonel. "What I don't understand is why you didn't tell an adult immediately. You had known for six hours that a German man, very probably a Nazi spy, was hiding in the barn. You and the other children must all have known perfectly well the correct procedure for reporting a suspicious person, and yet you chose to tell nobody. You decided instead to keep a watch on him yourselves, and then you took a loaded gun and crept out into the yard at night to shoot him. I can only assume that you were playing a silly childish game inspired by some gung-ho adventure story you'd been reading, imagining you were some kind of heroes."

Fury burned inside me. "Of course we weren't! I'm not stupid. You don't play games with Nazis."

"Very well." Colonel Ferguson stood up. He leaned across the desk, placing his palms flat on the polished wood. He regarded me in silence for a minute. Then he said, very quietly, "In that case, I think you have not told me the full story. I think there's something you're keeping from me. You are clearly an intelligent girl. You knew what this man was and what he might be capable of. You were very concerned to stop him doing any damage: so concerned, in fact, that you were prepared to kill him and face the consequences. And yet the one thing you should have done, and that you knew you should have done, was to report his presence immediately to a responsible adult. And that was the one thing you did not do."

He looked at me gravely. "I shall give you one more chance to tell the truth, Miss Schlesinger. I mean the whole truth, and nothing but the truth. And let me repeat, it will be far better for you and for the other children involved if you tell the truth now."

I couldn't hold his gaze. I looked at the floor. My stomach was an agony of cramps.

There was a horrible silence. Eventually I could bear it no longer.

"I promised I wouldn't tell," I whispered.

"Whom did you promise?"

I knew it sounded stupid. "Molly and Frank."

I glanced up at him. He raised his eyebrows. "I can assure you, Anna, that if you don't tell me the truth now, then Molly and Frank and their parents will be arrested and brought in for questioning immediately. Is that what you want?"

Still looking at the floor, I shook my head.

"Then tell me the truth."

CHAPTER THIRTY-FIVE

"Do Not Tell Him Anything"

If the Invader Comes

I was shaking. I had no option any more.

"Molly and Frank were talking in the barn before we knew the man was there. And Frank told Molly that Winston Churchill was coming here on Thursday."

The colonel's face paled. Private Willis made an outraged noise.

"From where had the boy received that information?" asked the colonel.

In my mind's eye I saw the kind, generous faces of Uncle Bert and Aunty Rose, and I felt like the world's worst traitor.

"That's the terrible thing, sir. Uncle Bert told Aunty Rose in secret."

The colonel made an impatient gesture. "Who are you talking about?"

"Sorry, sir. Mr and Mrs Dean, sir. My foster parents. Molly and Frank's parents."

"Go on."

"Mr Dean heard it from the butler at Ashcombe House. The butler said he'd been told to expect a very special visitor on Thursday, and he'd been asked to get a certain type of champagne and cigars, which he said were Mr Churchill's favourites. So he thought Mr Churchill must be coming here to inspect the troops on Thursday. Uncle Bert – Mr Dean – told it to Mrs Dean in secret. But he didn't know Frank was in the Anderson, and Frank overheard everything, and then he told Molly in the barn."

Private Willis gave an exclamation of disgust.

"Molly didn't know what Frank was going to tell her, and Frank's only seven. And they had no idea anyone else was in the barn. Once we knew he was German, we realised we'd given away a really important secret to the enemy. But Frank and Molly were frightened that if we reported him, and he said what he'd heard, then their dad would be arrested."

"Do you know exactly what Frank told Molly in the barn?" said Colonel Ferguson. "I mean *exactly*."

"Yes, sir. I asked them afterwards, and they told me every word. Molly has a really good memory."

"And can you tell me every word now?"

"Yes, sir."

I repeated the conversation exactly as Molly and Frank had told it to me. The colonel asked me to repeat it again, which I did.

"Judging by your account," said the colonel, after he'd heard it twice, "neither of the children mentioned the name of this village, or any other place name, during that conversation. Is that correct?"

"Yes, sir."

"You're absolutely certain of that?"

"Yes, sir. That's how we were able to trick him, sir."

The colonel continued to regard me in silence. Under his gaze, the icy-cold feeling crept over me again.

"You say there's another entrance to the barn?" he said. "An entrance that can't be seen from the loft?"

"Well, it's just a thin gap in the wall. We can get through it but a man wouldn't be able to."

"And apart from that, is there only one way in and out of the barn?"

"Yes, sir. The big main doors."

"Are there any windows, or gaps in the barn wall, from which this man could see the approach to those doors?"

I pictured the barn in my head. "There's only one window in the loft. It's on the opposite side to the door. It overlooks the lane to the village."

"Is the window big enough for a man to climb out?"

"No, it's just a little slit. It wouldn't even be big enough for me to climb out of."

The colonel started pacing up and down the long room, his eyes on the floor. Then he stopped pacing and wheeled round to face Private Willis.

"Escort Miss Schlesinger back to her house, Willis."

I stared at him. Was this the end of it? What would happen now?

"What about the man, sir?" I asked. "Shouldn't I go back and guard him?"

"Certainly not. Private Willis, Miss Schlesinger will show you the barn, and you will guard the entrance until relieved. I shall arrange for a guard to be permanently stationed there from now on."

The soldier saluted. "Yes, sir."

"But what shall I tell the others?" I asked. "I'm supposed to wake Molly at midnight. She'll want to know why I didn't wake her."

The colonel ignored me.

"Thank you for your valuable service this evening, Willis. You may rest assured it will not go unnoticed."

The soldier's face almost broke into a smile. "Thank you very much, sir," he said.

"Wait outside for a minute, will you?" the colonel said to him. "I need to have a word with Miss Schlesinger."

"Yes, sir."

Private Willis saluted and left the room. Once the door had closed behind him, Colonel Ferguson sat at his desk again. He gave me an intensely serious look.

"Everything that I am about to tell you," he said, "is of the utmost importance to our national security. Can I trust you to follow my instructions to the letter?"

"Of course."

"Listen very carefully. When Molly questions you in the morning as to why you didn't wake her, you will tell her that when you left the barn at midnight, a soldier was patrolling the yard near the barn door. He was suspicious as to what you were doing in the yard. You told him you had been looking after

201

a sick animal in the barn. You didn't wake Molly because you knew the man in the barn wouldn't be able to escape with a soldier stationed outside, and you didn't want the soldier's suspicions to be further aroused by the appearance of another child in the yard in the middle of the night."

He paused and looked hard at me. "Have you got that?"

"Yes, sir."

"Take the man food and water in the morning, exactly as you arranged, using the main entrance to the barn. Make absolutely sure that Mr and Mrs Dean don't notice or suspect anything out of the ordinary."

"Yes, sir."

"There will be a soldier stationed near the door of the barn. He will know who you are. Do not speak to him. Warn the other children not to speak to him either. If anybody speaks to him, the man in the barn will be alerted to his presence."

"But, sir – I mean, excuse me, sir, but what about all the farm workers, and Uncle Bert and Aunty Rose, and the farmer? There's always lots of people at the farm. They'll all see the soldier, and they'll probably speak to him."

"Everybody in the area will be informed that, for reasons of national security, extra troops will be stationed at various points around the village," said the colonel. "People will be asked not to speak to or otherwise distract the soldiers on guard duty. Your job, Miss Schlesinger, is as follows. If the man gives you a letter to post, or anything else to deliver anywhere, you must bring it straight to me. It is vitally important that you do this. Do you understand?"

"Yes, sir."

"Give your name to the duty soldiers at the main gates, and I'll make sure they'll be expecting you."

"Won't it look a bit strange though, sir, me walking up the drive for no reason? Should I bring some eggs with me? Then I can look as though I'm just delivering eggs to the house. We sell eggs around the village, you see."

The colonel looked much more cheerful all of a sudden. He rubbed his hands together happily. "That's a thoroughly good idea. And I'll be very happy to buy as many eggs as you can sell me. Marvellous."

Then he gave me a stern look. "It's of the utmost importance though, Miss Schlesinger, that absolutely nobody has any idea that you are doing this. And that includes the other two children. There must be nobody else involved at all. Is that quite clear?"

"Yes, sir."

I didn't know how I was going to keep this secret from Molly and Frank, but I would have to find a way. It wasn't going to be easy.

The colonel strode to the door and ushered me out.

"Thank you, Willis," he said. "Escort Miss Schlesinger home and stay at your post until relieved."

The soldier saluted. "Yes, sir."

"Can I have Uncle Bert's gun back?" I asked.

The colonel handed the gun to Private Willis.

"Lock it up again as soon as you get home," he told me.

"Yes, sir."

We left the room. As Private Willis closed the door, I heard Colonel Ferguson pick up the telephone.

CHAPTER THIRTY-SIX

"Do Not Give Any German Anything"

If the Invader Comes

Peter Smith shoved me against the living-room wall.

"What is your name?" he shouted. Saliva sprayed from his mouth and landed in my eyes. I tried to wipe my face but he slapped my hand away.

"What is your name?" he yelled again.

I tried to reply. My mouth formed the words, but no sound came out.

"Are you dumb as well as stupid, filthy Jew?" He smacked me in the face.

With a jolt of horror I saw my mother and father. They were huddled in a corner of the living room, dressed in rags, gagged and bound. I felt sick with guilt. Why hadn't I seen them before?

Their mouths were moving and I knew they were calling to me, but I couldn't hear their voices. The more they struggled and tried to shout, the less substantial they became, as though they were vanishing into a mist. And it was all my fault.

"What is your name? What is your name?" He was yelling it over and over, and each time he yelled it, he slapped my face, first one side and then the other.

"Anna Schlesinger," I tried to say, but no sound came out of my mouth. An SS officer appeared and dragged my parents out of the room. They reached out their arms to me. "Help us, Anna," they mouthed. "Help us."

I screamed, but still no sound came out, and I watched helplessly, writhing in Peter Smith's grasp, as they were dragged into another room and the door was kicked shut behind them.

"Anna, wake up!"

I screamed and thrashed my arms, but something was holding me tight. "Anna, it's all right. You've had a nightmare. It was just a bad dream, that's all."

I opened my eyes, my heart pounding. The sheet was wound around me like a shroud. I was soaked in sweat. Molly's hands were on my shoulders. She looked frightened.

"Are you all right?" she asked.

I nodded. I just wanted to forget it as soon as possible and be back in the real world. My parents were safe. At least, a Red Cross letter had come last week, so they had been all right when it was sent.

"It's seven o'clock," whispered Molly urgently. "What happened? Why didn't you wake me?"

My insides dissolved as last night's events flooded into my nightmare-addled head. Had that really happened?

"Anna, wake up!" Molly whispered urgently. "What time did you come back? Why didn't you wake me?"

I rubbed my face and sat up. "It's all right. There's

a soldier guarding him."

Molly went white. "What do you mean? How do they know? Did you tell them? What's happening?"

"Molly, please. Stop asking questions and I'll tell you. But it's best if Frank hears it at the same time. Let's all go to the tree house."

Once we were safely in the tree house, I told them exactly what Colonel Ferguson had told me to tell them.

"But why's there a soldier stationed in the farmyard?" asked Molly. "It's a bit odd. Do you think they know the man's here?"

My stomach churned.

"They can't do," said Frank. "If they knew he was here, they'd just arrest him."

"I expect it's just general security precautions," I said, trying to speak lightly. "You know, national defences, that sort of thing. I don't expect it's just here. They're probably putting more troops everywhere."

"Maybe because of you-know-who coming on Thursday," said Frank.

"Yes, probably," I said.

"Well, it's worked out really well, actually," said Molly. "Thank goodness we don't have to worry about guarding him any more."

"Just feeding him," I said. "We'll have to smuggle some food to him after breakfast."

"What about the soldier on duty?" said Frank. "Won't he be suspicious if we keep taking food to the barn?"

"We'll hide it in pockets or under our clothes,"

said Molly, "and if anyone asks about the water, we'll say we keep a bowl of water in the barn for Clover. Remember to pretend to be really hungry at breakfast, and save the extra slice of bread."

We walked back to the cottage in silence. What Frank and Molly had said had got me thinking. Why *hadn't* Colonel Ferguson just had the man arrested? Why let him stay in the barn and ask me to hand over his letters?

It could only be because the colonel wanted to read those letters. And that must mean he suspected the man was part of a wider network of spies. So he wanted to read his letters secretly and learn as much as he could about the other spies in the network: where they were located and what they were planning to do. Then, at the right moment, they would all be arrested.

That must be it, mustn't it?

I just hoped Colonel Ferguson knew what he was doing.

CHAPTER THIRTY-SEVEN

"If You See Anything Suspicious, Note It Carefully"

If the Invader Comes

"We're sorry there's no jam," Molly said to the man, as we took our smuggled slices of bread out from under our shirts and handed them to him, "but we can't make Mum suspicious, you see."

"Thank you," said the man, taking a huge bite of bread. "I am very hungry. Will you be able to go to a shop this morning?"

"Yes, I think so," said Molly.

"Would you please post this letter for me?" he said, taking an envelope from his pocket.

Molly held out her hand for it, but the man drew it closer to his chest. The envelope was addressed and stamped, but not sealed.

"I have one more part to add to the letter, and I wondered if you children could help me."

My stomach was a mass of nerves.

"Of course," said Molly. "If we can."

"I would like my mother to be able to reply, since I might be here for a few more days. But I cannot of course ask her to send a letter to me in this barn."

"You could ask her to send it to us," said Frank. "Then we could pass it on to you."

209

"Don't be stupid," Molly said. "We never get letters. It would look pretty suspicious if we suddenly started getting secret communications from a stranger."

"What if she sent it to Anna?" asked Frank. "She gets letters."

"Not with a Kent postmark."

"I have an idea," I said.

Three pairs of eyes turned to me.

"What about Mrs Chantrey's address? She's moving to Scotland tomorrow, isn't she? And she's given your mum a key to her cottage, to keep an eye on things until her tenants move in. What if we offer to water her plants and send on her post, to save your mum a job? If Peter's mother wrote to that address, we could go round every morning when the post arrives and bring his letters here."

"That's a brilliant idea," said Frank.

Even the man looked impressed.

With the man's eyes fixed on my face, there was no way I could signal to Molly and Frank. I would just have to rely on them following my train of thought.

"She lives in a little village called Ashcombe. It's several miles away, but we can cycle there."

I held my breath, ready to jump in and talk over Frank if he questioned me. But his face was impressively blank.

"How will we know which letter is from Peter's mother though?" said Molly. "We can't bring him all Mrs Chantrey's post. We need to forward her real letters to her new address."

"What if, when you write the address down now for your mother," I said, "you spell one of the words wrong. Not badly wrong, but enough to make it a sign for us."

"You are a clever girl," said the man, and the way he looked at me made my skin crawl.

"So which word should he spell wrong?" Frank asked.

"Mrs Chantrey lives on Neaves Lane," said Molly. "N-E-A-V-E-S. So, Peter, you write it down as N-E-E-V-E-S. Then we'll know that any letters with that spelling are from your mother, and we'll bring them straight round."

The man drew the letter out of the envelope and unfolded it. "Could you tell me the exact name and address that my mother should write to, please?"

I crouched down next to him, as though I was being friendly. "The name is Mrs Chantrey."

"That's spelt C-H-A-N-T-R-E-Y," said Molly slowly. I glanced at her. Was she being extra slow in order to give me more time to read the letter?

I watched him write as Molly spelled out the address. I pretended to be checking that he was writing the address down correctly. To my surprise, he had spread the paper out quite openly, making no attempt to cover up what he had written.

I was even more surprised when I scanned the writing. It really was a letter to his mother. He talked about his concerns for her health, his desire to see her and his frustration at being delayed because of his injury.

For a moment, I wondered whether we'd been wrong about him after all. Had we let our imaginations run away with us? Perhaps he really was a British soldier who just wanted to visit his sick mother.

But of course he wasn't. He spoke German when he thought he was alone, and he had a wireless transmitter he was trying to fix. Well, we didn't actually know it was a wireless transmitter, but he was certainly trying to fix some sort of machine that he was hiding from us.

The letter must be in code. Either that or he was using invisible ink. I scrutinised the paper, but if it was invisible ink then it was completely invisible. I looked at the first letter of every word in the opening sentence, in case it spelled out a message, but the letters read DMIHYAFB.

"Is that all correct?" he asked, when he had written down Mrs Chantrey's address.

"Perfect," I said.

He licked the envelope, sealed it and passed it to Molly, who tucked it into her trouser pocket.

How was I going to find a way to take the letter to Colonel Ferguson?

"Will you be able to post it immediately?" the man asked. "My mother will be worried that I have not yet arrived."

"Of course," Molly reassured him. "We'll take it straightaway. Don't worry, we know it's important."

It must be a good sign, I suddenly realised, that he was so keen to get his letter sent off. It must mean he hadn't got his transmitter working.

"How's your ankle today?" Frank asked.

"I think it's getting better. The pain is less. After I have eaten, I shall try to walk a little. It may be that I can leave for my mother's house tomorrow."

"Oh, I shouldn't try that," said Molly. "You don't want to damage your ankle more by walking on it before it's ready. I think you'd be best to leave it until it's properly healed."

"Anyway," I said, "I'm afraid you can't leave at the moment. There are soldiers patrolling the yard."

He jerked his head up in alarm. I hadn't planned to say that, but we couldn't let him escape.

"Soldiers? Here?"

We nodded.

"They patrol the perimeter fence," said Molly, "and since last night there's been one in the yard too. Well, not the same one all the time. They work in shifts."

"Why did you not tell me this?" he snapped. "Why is there a soldier here? What does he do? Do they suspect something? Have you given anything away?" Suddenly he sat bolt upright. "Did he see you come into the barn?"

Molly sat beside him and gave him a kind smile. "Don't worry. They don't suspect anything. We talked to one of them and he said it's just a routine security measure, since there are troops stationed on the estate."

"But did he see you come to the barn?" he hissed. He looked very tense, every muscle strained.

"We told him our cat lives in here," said Molly, "so we come to feed her and play with her."

"And she does sort of live here," said Frank. "So that's all right."

"So when they see us bring water to the barn," said Molly, "they'll think it's for Clover, you see. But you mustn't go out at the moment, all right? Just stay and rest your ankle. Your mother will know you've been delayed when she gets the letter, won't she?"

"You will have to distract the duty soldier," he said, "to give me the opportunity to get away."

"Yes," agreed Molly. "We'll do that. But not yet. You need to rest your ankle and we need to post your letter."

We said goodbye and didn't speak again until we were back in the tree house. Then Molly took the envelope out of her pocket.

The address said:

Mrs Jean Smith,
Oyster Cottage,
Beach Walk,
Whitstable,
Kent

"It looks so ordinary, doesn't it?" said Molly. "What did the letter say?"

"It looked completely normal. Just like a letter a soldier would write to his mother. There were one or two odd words in it, but I couldn't tell whether that's just his way of writing, or because he was needing to use those words to fit into some sort of code."

"It's bound to be in code," said Molly. "Unless he's used a very good invisible ink. Just think, inside this envelope there might be instructions to bomb Muddle Green."

"Or shoot Winston Churchill," said Frank.

"Or both," said Molly.

"So what should we do with it?" asked Frank.

"Burn it," said Molly.

"No!" I said, before I could stop myself.

Molly frowned at me. "Of course we have to burn it. If anyone finds it and cracks the code, this letter could get Dad hanged for treason."

"But..." I said, frantically trying to think of something, anything that would convince Molly. "We can't just burn it. That might be treason too. Think about it. Destroying evidence. That's a really serious crime."

"So what do you suggest?" asked Molly.

"I think we should just keep it hidden for the moment. If you think about it, it doesn't look suspicious, does it? It just looks like a letter to someone called Mrs Jean Smith in Whitstable."

"It'll look pretty suspicious if Mum finds it. How can we explain it? And there's nowhere to hide anything in our house. She's bound to find it sooner or later."

"Unless..." I said, as an idea suddenly struck me. "Unless I tuck it in the box with all my letters. Aunty Rose would never dream of snooping about in there. She knows how precious those letters are to me."

I had the satisfaction of seeing Molly flush bright red. Good. She still felt bad about what she'd done. I didn't want her to think for one moment that I'd forgiven her, just because we were having to work together at the moment.

"That's perfect," said Frank.

"I'm not sure," said Molly. "I still think we should burn it."

"Why?" I asked, giving her my most piercing look. "Don't you trust your mother? Do you think she's the kind of person who would secretly rummage around in somebody else's most treasured possessions?"

Molly looked away from me. "No," she said.

"Do you think your dad is the kind of person who would do that?"

"Of course not."

"So then it will be completely safe, won't it?"

"I suppose so."

"That's settled then."

And I took the letter and put it in my pocket.

CHAPTER THIRTY-EIGHT

"Remember Parachutists Are Powerless Against Organised Resistance"

If the Invader Comes

I gave my name to the duty soldiers at the main gates, and then I carried the basket of eggs along the leafy avenue, keeping my head to the ground and taking deep breaths to control the sick, panicky feeling as I passed the hordes of troops doing drills and exercises.

I gave my name again to the duty soldiers at the foot of the main steps, trying not to look at their guns. One of them nodded and escorted me around the side of the house, exactly as had happened last night. Now I saw we were walking through the stable yard. The brick-built stables formed three sides of a large square, with the house on my right forming the fourth side. A big group of soldiers was marching and drilling in the yard, while an officer shouted orders. I kept my eyes on the ground, but I saw bayonets glinting in the sunlight, and that sight combined with the shouting and the sound of their boots on the cobbles made me dizzy with panic. I put my hand on the house wall to steady myself. My breath came out in shudders.

It's all right, I told myself. *It's all right. They're not*

Nazis. They won't hurt you. It's all right.

"Are you all right?" asked the soldier escorting me.

I nodded. He waited while I took a couple more breaths and gingerly took my hand away from the wall. Then he approached the soldier guarding the side door. "Anna Schlesinger, to see Colonel Ferguson," he said.

The man on guard opened the door and instructed another soldier, who was stationed in the corridor, to escort Miss Schlesinger to Colonel Ferguson's office.

I felt slightly calmer inside the house. The soldier knocked on Colonel Ferguson's door and stepped inside to announce my arrival.

"Send her in," said the colonel.

The soldier indicated for me to enter the room and then he left.

The colonel strode across to greet me. My stomach churned. He was wearing battledress.

"Good morning, Miss Schlesinger," he said. "Come in. Ah, you brought the eggs. Marvellous."

I was startled to see another man standing behind the colonel's desk. He was older than the colonel, and he wore a civilian suit and tie, with a very white shirt. A metre or so away from the desk, a smartly-dressed young woman with dark wavy hair sat on a straight-backed chair. She held a pencil and had a spiral-bound notebook open on her knee.

Were they here for some other reason, or were they interested in Peter Smith's letter too?

Colonel Ferguson closed the door and carried a

second chair over to his desk. Both men sat down behind the desk. The colonel motioned for me to sit on the empty chair facing them.

My heart gave a nasty lurch. Had this man been brought in to interrogate me? Was it all a trap? Were they going to arrest me?

I sat down, feeling cold all over.

"Anna, this is Mr Rivers," said the colonel. "I telephoned him last night after our conversation and relayed to him all that you told me. He is very interested in the man you discovered in your barn. Did the man give you anything this morning?"

I handed him the letter. "He gave us this. He asked us to post it to his mother."

The colonel handed it to Mr Rivers, who examined the envelope very closely from all angles. Then he walked to a door in the panelled wall that I hadn't noticed before. He gave a sharp knock and, without waiting for an answer, opened the door. I tried to see what was inside the room. It seemed to be a sort of inner office. I glimpsed a tall filing cabinet and a cork board on the wall above it, on which were pinned several sheets of paper.

I couldn't see anybody in the room, but there must have been somebody there, because Mr Rivers stepped inside and said, "Telephone through to HQ and have a watch put on this address immediately. Then start on the letter."

I heard a mumbled reply but I couldn't make out any words. Mr Rivers came out, closed the door behind him and sat next to the colonel. He drew the chair closer to the desk and leaned his elbows on the polished surface. Resting his chin on his clasped hands, he gave me a very direct look. I got the feeling that he was the kind of person who would know immediately if you weren't telling the truth.

"The man you discovered in your barn," he said. "I want you to tell me the whole story, please, from the moment you discovered him. I realise that you told the colonel last night, but I need to hear it first-hand. Miss Johnson, my stenographer, will take notes."

I told him everything, being very careful to try to remember every detail in the correct order. Mr Rivers listened attentively, while Miss Johnson scribbled on her pad. Occasionally Mr Rivers interrupted to ask for clarification on a point, but mostly he just let me talk.

When I finished, he turned to the colonel.

"Does Miss Schlesinger's account match the one she gave you last night?" he asked.

The colonel nodded. "No discrepancies at all."

"Thank you, Miss Schlesinger," said Mr Rivers. "You may go. I need hardly tell you that you are not, of course, to mention a word of our conversation to anybody outside this room."

"And what do we do about the man?" I asked.

"Do?"

"Yes. We have to carry on taking him food and water, or he'll suspect he's been found out. Shouldn't we try to destroy his transmitter too?"

Mr Rivers gripped the edge of the desk.

"Absolutely not. You are not to try anything of the sort. This man is extremely dangerous. I'm not happy with you associating with him at all, but since you've got yourselves into this situation, it's probably the best course of action to continue taking him food and water. Be polite, give nothing away and let us do the rest."

"If he's so dangerous," I said, "then why don't you just arrest him straightaway?"

Nobody said anything. Mr Rivers looked at the desk.

"Is it because you think he might be part of a spy ring, and you want to flush out the other spies?"

Mr Rivers gave me a startled look and I knew I'd guessed correctly.

"It is, isn't it? He's part of a spy ring. Are they planning something big?"

"I'm afraid I cannot give you classified information," he said.

"You're from the Secret Service, aren't you?"

He opened his eyes wider.

"Why don't you use me? I could help you."

"Help me?"

"Yes. To trap the spy ring."

The colonel smiled and frowned at the same time, an expression I hadn't realised was possible.

"I'm serious," I said. "We've been deceiving this man since yesterday afternoon, haven't we? He clearly trusts us or he wouldn't have given us a letter. And we've arranged to intercept the replies too."

Mr Rivers started. "You've done what?"

I told him how we had used Mrs Chantrey's address, and the misspelling that would enable us to identify the letters sent to the man. "So if you want to catch the spies, I could pass his letters to you, and pass messages and information to him that would help you trap the others in his spy ring."

Mr Rivers looked at me. Then his gaze moved to the wall behind me. He seemed to be thinking. Nobody moved.

Eventually he stood up. "I need to speak to Colonel Ferguson alone."

"I'll wait outside," I said.

Mr Rivers turned to the colonel and asked, "Is there another room where Miss Schlesinger can wait?"

The colonel nodded. He led me out of the room and indicated a door on the opposite side of the hall. There didn't seem to be anybody around. All the soldiers must have been out on manoeuvres or doing drills.

I crossed the hall and went into the other room, closing the door. I waited until I heard Colonel Ferguson's door shut behind him, and then I carefully opened the door and crept back across the hall. I peered through the keyhole. The two men were standing in front of the fireplace. When I put my ear to the keyhole, I could hear them clearly.

"...by far the simplest solution," the colonel was saying.

"It may be the simplest solution at the moment," said Mr Rivers, "but that's not the point. It's about strategy. We have to make him useful to us."

"If you brought him in now," said the colonel, "would he turn, do you think?"

Mr Rivers shook his head. "Not a chance. He won't turn. A lot of them will – some of them turn straightaway – but not 'Peter Smith', as he calls himself. We've been following his movements for a while. He's a fanatical Nazi. Devoted to Hitler and the Third Reich."

I had that hollowed-out feeling again. My legs shook. I steadied myself against the doorframe.

"We were pretty sure he was in England," said Mr Rivers, "but we had no idea where. And clearly his transmitter's broken, so we had no signals to intercept. It's an incredible piece of luck, those children coming across him and seeing through his cover story."

"Well, if you're sure he won't turn, and you want to use him to flush out the others," said the colonel, "wouldn't it make sense to do as the girl suggests, and use her? After all, how else are you going to feed him information? You can hardly send him letters addressed to Peter Smith, The Hayloft in the Barn. And you can't exactly go and have a chat with him yourself."

"We can't use a child," Mr Rivers said. "It would bring the whole Service into disrepute."

"Jolly good idea, though, when you think about it," said the colonel. "Who's going to suspect her of being a secret agent for the British government?"

"It wouldn't be ethical. She doesn't know what

she's getting herself into."

The colonel's voice turned serious. "Stanford, you've read Anna's records. She spent six years of her life as a Jewish girl in Hitler's Germany. She had her home destroyed by Nazi thugs. Her father was sent to a concentration camp. Her family lost their business. She brought an unregistered baby on the Kindertransport, facing down the SS and standing up to the Dutch authorities. If anyone knows what they're getting themselves into, it's her."

I couldn't help it; my legs gave way and I collapsed on the floor in a cold sweat. How did these men know all that?

The door opened wide. Two tall figures looked down at me.

I'd ruined everything. There was no way they'd let me work for them now.

I scrambled into a sitting position. I didn't trust myself to stand yet.

There was a horrible silence. Then Colonel Ferguson said, "You'd better come in."

CHAPTER THIRTY-NINE

"Think Always of Your Country Before You Think of Yourself"

If the Invader Comes

Feeling cold and sweaty, I walked back into the room. Colonel Ferguson motioned for me to sit in front of the desk again, and asked Miss Johnson to fetch a cup of tea.

"And a biscuit, if you can find one," he called after her.

The men sat behind the desk.

"So," said the colonel, "you were listening at the door. I suppose you heard every word we said, did you?"

My heart was thumping, but I knew there was no point in lying.

"I heard from when you were talking about whether he would turn, and Mr Rivers said he wouldn't because he's a fanatical Nazi."

"I see."

"You can trust me. I won't say a word."

Mr Rivers leaned forward.

"Anna, before I came here this morning, I called in at Bloomsbury House. Having heard Colonel Ferguson's report on the telephone last night, I wanted to learn a bit about your background from the committee of the Refugee Children's Movement."

So that was how they knew about me.

"The ladies at Bloomsbury House were very keen to impress on me your exceptional character. They stressed how you looked after the other children on the train and the boat to England. They showed me a letter from one of the Dutch refugee workers at the Hook of Holland, who had been so impressed by your passionate protection of the baby you were looking after that she had felt moved to write a letter in praise of you to the Refugee Children's Movement. Your courage and resourcefulness are not in doubt, Anna, and neither is your evident desire to help the British war effort."

"Then let me help, please."

"As I said, your character and motives are not in doubt. My concerns are regarding your age and your particular circumstances. You are thirteen years old, and it is hardly necessary to say that we do not recruit children into the Secret Service. Secondly, and this is an even graver consideration, your parents sent you to this country to protect you. They wanted you to be safe, far away from Hitler's Germany. If I allowed you to become involved in our activities, then I would be putting you in potential danger, and I could not with a clear conscience allow that to happen."

I thought for a moment. Then I said, "I don't think I would really be in much danger." He opened his mouth to respond, so I hurried on. "I understand what you're saying, Mr Rivers, of course. I know he's armed and I know he's a Nazi. But he has no reason to hurt me, does he? In fact, it would be really stupid of him to hurt me. He doesn't want anybody to discover his hiding place, does he? He knows there's a soldier on duty outside. If anything happened to any of us, the duty soldier would know, and he'd be discovered. And surely it's in his interests to be nice to us. We're the only way for him to get food and water, for a start. And now we're taking his messages for him. As long as we're useful to him, then surely he's not going to harm us. If he's one of Germany's most dangerous spies, then presumably he must be clever. Surely he's clever enough to work out that it wouldn't help his cause if he harmed us."

The men looked at each other. A little smile played at the corner of the colonel's mouth.

"I say, Rivers. I think you've just been out-argued by a child."

Mr Rivers didn't smile back. He turned to me, looking very grave.

"To an extent, you are, of course, right. As long as you and your friends are useful to this man, he is very unlikely to hurt you. However..." He paused and looked intently at me. "However, if he believes that you are no longer useful to him, or if he suspects that you have any suspicions about who he really is, or if he suspects for any other reason that his cover has been blown or his life is in danger, then he will have no hesitation at all in using that gun."

He stopped. I sensed I shouldn't interrupt. I waited for him to continue.

"Over the first of those circumstances," he said, "we have a good level of control. We can make sure you're useful to him, by taking essential supplies, and by posting his letters and delivering the replies. Over the second circumstance – whether he suspects that you think he is not who he says he is – only you have control. You and your friends would have to keep up the pretence, at all times, whatever he says or does, that you think he is an ordinary English soldier who just wants to visit his sick mother. Do you think you are capable of that?"

"Yes," I said. "And I'll talk to Molly and Frank about it again. But they've done a really good job so far."

"Over the third circumstance," he said, "I and my colleagues have control. We will, of course, do everything we possibly can to keep our activities undetected. We will have our very best people on the job. But there is always an element of risk, and I would be deceiving you if I didn't make that clear. And I – we, all of the British people – have a duty to keep you safe. After the sacrifice your parents have made in sending you here, that is the least they deserve."

A feeling swelled within me. It was that feeling I had had twice before, once when looking after Ezra on the journey to England, and once when Molly and Frank were hysterical in the tree house after they realised they'd given away a state secret.

It was a feeling of power and determination.

"Mr Rivers," I said. "When I left for England,

my parents told me to be grateful to the British people, and they told me to be brave. They would be proud..." I was alarmed to find tears coming to my eyes. I swallowed. "They would be so proud if they thought I was helping the war effort. It's what they would want to do themselves, if they had the chance."

Mr Rivers looked at me for a long moment. Then he said, "When the letter you gave us has been examined, it will be posted. Expect a reply within the next few days. When it arrives, please bring it here immediately."

The colonel moved towards the door to usher me out. I felt like a different person. Taller. Stronger.

With this new feeling of strength, a thought occurred to me. I gathered all my courage into a tight knot of resolution and turned to face Mr Rivers.

"There's one more thing."

"Yes?"

"This is dangerous work, isn't it? This man is one of Germany's top spies, and he's armed."

"Yes." He looked a little uncomfortable.

"And I'm happy to do this work for you. But I want you to do one thing for me in return."

He frowned.

"You have to promise," I said, "that Molly's father won't get into trouble for what he said."

Mr Rivers was silent for a moment. Then he said, "That seems like a reasonable request."

"Oh, thank you!" I said. "Thank you so much."

CHAPTER FORTY

"The Ordinary Man and Woman Must Be on the Watch"
If the Invader Comes

I walked back down the avenue, feeling the wonderful lightness of relief. Uncle Bert was safe.

It was a pity I couldn't tell Frank. It was awful that a seven-year-old had to carry all that worry around with him.

The duty soldiers said, "Goodbye, miss," as I walked out of the gates. I said goodbye to them and turned towards the farm.

"So that's where you were."

I stopped in shock. Molly was standing in the lane. She looked furious.

"What have you been up to, sneaking off behind my back?"

My heart started beating very fast. "What do you mean, sneaking off behind your back? I don't need your permission to leave the house."

"I knew you were up to something. You said you'd help Mum with the Saucepans into Spitfires collection, and you always help when you say you will."

I stared at her. "So you *followed* me?"

"I had to find out what you were up to. It's not a

game. It's my dad's life."

I glared at her. "So stop discussing it in the middle of the street, idiot."

"There's no one around."

I gave a bitter laugh. "That's what you thought in the barn yesterday. And look where that's got us."

She shot me a look of mingled fury and pain.

"You're really horrible sometimes, Anna, you know that?"

Seeing the hurt in her face actually did make me feel bad. After all, yesterday had been Frank's fault, not hers.

"Fine," I said. "We'll discuss it in the usual place."

She quickened her pace until she was walking several metres ahead of me. I slowed my pace to increase the gap. I needed some thinking time.

Molly was waiting in the tree house. I could see she was fizzing with rage. I had barely stepped off the ladder when she whispered furiously, "You betrayed me. How dare you betray me?"

I gave a bitter laugh. "*I* betrayed *you*? What, by leaving the farm without telling you? How is that a betrayal?"

"Don't try and pretend, Anna. You've been up at the army camp. You can't deny it. I saw the soldiers saying goodbye to you, all matey like you were old friends. What were you doing?"

"Delivering eggs."

"Oh, please! We don't even sell eggs there."

"Some of the soldiers asked if they could buy eggs,

231

so I took some."

"If that's true, why would you not tell Mum or me about it? You know Mum can't just start selling eggs to new customers. There wouldn't be enough for her regulars. And I know you wouldn't sell eggs behind her back. So stop lying to me. What were you actually doing?"

I looked away. What could I say? Molly's face was a mixture of anger and fear. She must be really worried that whatever I was doing would get her dad in terrible trouble.

But I didn't owe her anything. She had betrayed me in the worst possible way. And she had got us into this trouble in the first place. Well, Frank had. And anyway, how could I possibly tell her the truth, even if I wanted to? I'd made a promise to the army and the Secret Service. Promises don't get more serious than that.

"I know you're up to something, Anna. I knew something was going on when you were so against burning his letter. Why would you want to keep it in the box with your parents' letters? Why would you *not* want to burn it? Something's going on and I'm not going to let you go until you tell me what it is."

"I'm never going to tell you. Why should I tell you anything? How can I trust you, when you don't trust me?"

"I do trust you. I trust you completely. I know you're on our side. I know you don't want Dad to get in trouble. But I also know you're doing things you're not telling me about, and I have to know. It's about my family, after all."

I looked at her agonised face. I knew what it felt like to worry constantly about my father's safety. And I did really want to set Molly's mind at rest. Partly for her, of course, but I have to admit it was mainly for me. I was proud I'd thought of making that bargain with Mr Rivers. It felt like an achievement. And I wanted Molly to know about it.

"All right," I said. "But only if you swear, as the most solemn promise you've ever made, that you won't breathe a word of this to anybody, ever. Not even Frank."

Molly's eyes were wide with anticipation.

"All right," she said. "I solemnly swear."

CHAPTER FORTY-ONE

"Try to Give Exact Information"
If the Invader Comes

So I told her everything. She listened in entranced silence until I reached the point where I'd told Colonel Ferguson what Uncle Bert had said to Aunty Rose about Churchill's visit. Her face paled.

"No! How could you? How dare you! After all he's—"

"They've promised your dad won't get in trouble."

She stared at me. "They? Who? How?"

"I told Mr Rivers that if he wanted me to do this dangerous work for him, he had to promise your dad wouldn't get in trouble for what he said."

"And he agreed?"

"We're doing really important war work, aren't we? Thanks to us, they know the location of a spy they've been trying to track down for ages. Now they've got him under guard, *and* we're delivering his messages to them so they can decode them and locate the rest of his spy ring."

"We're secret agents!" said Molly. "We're actually secret agents!"

Then she looked at me awkwardly. She frowned and looked down at her hands. She bit her lip and

234

picked at her fingernails.

"That was nice, the way you said 'we'," she said eventually.

"What are you talking about?"

"When you said we're doing important war work. We. Like we're working together."

I shrugged. "We are working together. We don't really have a choice, do we?"

"Well, it's nice of you to say it. And thank you for making them promise that Dad wouldn't get in trouble. It was really nice of you to sort the situation out, especially when none of it was your fault."

"It wasn't your fault either."

"No, but Frank's my brother."

She paused, looking down at her fidgeting hands again. I could tell she was working up to saying something, so I waited in silence. The silence lasted ages.

"Listen, Anna," she said finally. "I'm so, so sorry about taking your letter into school. I'm so sorry about ever taking any notice of Billy's stupid ideas. I hate myself every day for being so stupid. I don't know why I did it. I was such an idiot. I think..." She shook her head. "Oh, I don't know."

"What? What were you going to say? You think what?"

She shook her head again. "Nothing. It sounds so stupid."

"Just say it."

"All right. I think... Maybe I was jealous."

"Jealous! Of me!"

"Mum and Dad think you're wonderful, and Frank loves you, and you're so clever, and Miss Marshall thinks you're perfect, and... Oh, you see, it sounds so pathetic, doesn't it? I'm just a horrible person."

I looked at her face, all screwed up and miserable, and all of a sudden I didn't hate her any more.

"You're not a horrible person," I said. "You've been really nice to me ever since I came, apart from that one thing. You were so helpful and patient with teaching me English. You shared all your friends with me and made sure they were my friends too. You even came with me to Ashcombe House to help me get jobs for my parents. And you've never made a fuss about sharing your room."

"Well, I was sharing with Frank before, anyway."

"Even so. It's different, sharing your room with a stranger. And sharing your parents too. I wouldn't have liked that."

"Really?" She looked up then, and there was a glimmer of hope on her face.

"No. I'd have hated having to share my parents with a stranger. And I understand why you find it annoying that I like helping in the house, and that I get good marks at school. But honestly, Molly, you should never, ever be jealous of me. It wouldn't make any difference if I helped in the house every moment of every day: Aunty Rose is still your mum, not mine. You've got a mum and a dad and a brother, and you live in the same house as them, and they'll always love you, whatever happens, because they're your family. And the reason I work hard at school and want to do well is because that's all I've got. The Nazis took away my father's business, and they destroyed all our things, and I don't even get proper letters any more. I have no idea what my parents' lives are like. I don't even know if they have enough to eat. I worry about them every single day and there's nothing I can do to help, and if Hitler invades England and the Germans win the war, then I'll never be safe again and I'll probably never see my parents again."

I was crying now, and I didn't even try to stop. "So yes, you are stupid. Really stupid." For some reason, I started laughing through my tears: a weird, slightly hysterical laugh. "You're really stupid. Being jealous of me is the most stupid thing you've ever done."

Molly held out her arms and drew me into a hug. I didn't pull away from her. I just sobbed on her shoulder until her shirt was soaked with tears.

CHAPTER FORTY-TWO

"When the Danger Comes Nearer"

If the Invader Comes

We went to Mrs Chantrey's cottage that day and the next, even though we knew there was no possibility of the man receiving a reply to his letter until Tuesday. But Aunty Rose had been very pleased when we offered to check the cottage for her. "Just don't go touching any of her things, will you?" she said, as she handed us the keys. "Water the plants and collect the post, that's all."

On Tuesday we walked to Neaves Lane just after the postman had made his morning rounds. As we opened the front door, our eyes immediately fell on a letter, lying on the doormat. Molly snatched it up and I felt the hairs stand up on my arms as we read the second line of the address.

Neeves Lane.

"Right," said Molly. "You'd better take this to Ashcombe House."

Colonel Ferguson lifted the speckled brown eggs from the hay-lined basket and placed them carefully on his desk. Then I took the letter from under the hay. Mr Rivers scrutinised the address before taking it to the inner office. The colonel gave me the money for the eggs and I put it in the basket.

Mr Rivers emerged from the office empty-handed.

"What shall I do about the letter?" I asked. "I have to take it to the man, or he'll get suspicious."

"Can you bring more eggs this afternoon and collect it then?" asked Mr Rivers.

"Aunty Rose will notice if I take any more eggs. But I could bring jam. She's been making loads of jam."

The colonel's face lit up. "Jam would be excellent."

"Come at two o'clock," said Mr Rivers. "Then you can take the letter to Mr Smith as though it arrived in the afternoon post."

Molly volunteered to help her mum with the Saucepans into Spitfires collection, and Frank was keen to help too, so it was easy for me to make another trip to Ashcombe House that afternoon. I took a pot of strawberry jam in the basket and received the letter back in exchange.

I scrutinised both sides of the envelope before tucking it under the hay. You would never have known it had been opened. I wondered how they did it. Did they steam it open, or did they have a special chemical that dissolved the glue on the envelope?

I waited for Molly to return before taking the letter to the man. I told myself I was waiting because I knew she'd want to be involved, but it was also because I hated the thought of being alone with him.

As we pushed the door open and the light streamed

into the barn, a thud came from the loft, as though something heavy had fallen on the floor. Then there were scrabbling sounds. We shot puzzled looks at each other before climbing the ladder.

The man looked jittery and nervous. He almost snatched the letter out of Molly's hand.

"Are you hungry?" asked Molly. "Do you need more water?"

"No, no," he said impatiently. Then he seemed to remember his manners. "Forgive me. It is just that I am so worried about my mother."

He was fingering the envelope, clearly desperate to open it.

"Of course," said Molly. "We'll leave you in peace. I hope your mother's feeling better."

She started to climb down the ladder.

"When will you be back?" he asked.

Molly's head was level with the loft floor. "We'll bring you something to eat this evening."

"Good. I shall write a reply to my mother. Would you be so kind as to post it this evening?"

"Of course. We're glad to help."

CHAPTER FORTY-THREE

"You Must Not Be Taken by Surprise"
If the Invader Comes

Wednesday seemed to drag on forever. It was so horrible to think the man in the barn was probably plotting to cause some unknown act of destruction the very next day.

"I have tried to walk," he told us on Wednesday evening, when we took him bread and cheese. "But it is still useless." He gestured in frustration at his ankle. "I think it must be broken. If it were a simple sprain, surely it would have healed by now."

Molly nodded. "I think you're right. What a shame. That might take a long time to heal. Your poor mother. How is she?"

The man shook his head sadly. "She is very unwell."

"That must be such a worry for you. She'll be so pleased to see you when you manage to get to her. Do you have a letter you'd like us to post?"

"Not tonight. I am tired now. I need to sleep."

"No letters," I whispered, when we were safely in our room. "Do you think that means their plans are fixed?"

241

Molly shuddered. "I really hope Mr Rivers knows what he's doing."

That night I had the nightmare about Peter Smith and my parents again. And there was no relief when I woke up. Thursday had come at last, and I felt dizzy with fear.

"Are you all right, Anna?" asked Aunty Rose at the breakfast table. "You've hardly eaten anything."

"Sorry. I've got a bit of a headache."

"You do look pale. Fresh air will sort you out. I've got a list of errands in the village you can run for me, as soon as you've had some breakfast."

"I'll come with you," said Molly.

"No, I need you in the house. There's all those blackcurrants want doing for jam. Anna's perfectly capable of going to the village on her own."

I walked back home along the lane, carrying Aunty Rose's shopping basket and trying not to think about what might be happening in Muddle Green right now.

It's all right, I reassured myself. We've intercepted all his letters. Mr Rivers knows what they're planning. He'll have people following them. They'll catch them before they can do anything.

But I still had to force myself to breathe normally.

The duty soldiers at the entrance to Ashcombe Park said hello to me as I walked past the gates. The Park was strangely quiet today. Usually the grass was swarming with men doing drills and exercises.

Were they out on manoeuvres? But I hadn't seen or heard convoys of army lorries.

Then, with a lurch in my stomach, I realised. It must be because of Churchill's visit. If he was coming to inspect the troops, then maybe they would all be lined up on parade somewhere in the grounds. It would be the perfect opportunity for Nazi saboteurs to plant a bomb and cause maximum damage.

Well, at least the soldiers would be safe here. I just hoped Peter Smith's associates would be caught before they could cause any damage in Muddle Green.

As I passed a gateway, a movement in the hedge on the other side of the field caught my eye. The hedgerow was thick and overgrown, but there were a few patches where the vegetation thinned out. And a shadowy figure was moving through one of these patches.

My heart beat faster. I drew back behind the gatepost, keeping my eyes fixed on a small gap in the hedge just ahead of where I'd seen the figure. Whoever it was would have to pass through that gap.

The shadow disappeared into thick foliage. I waited. And then a head appeared in the gap.

Peter Smith's head.

CHAPTER FORTY-FOUR

"Think Before You Act"

If the Invader Comes

I stood there, frozen, heart racing, head spinning.

He crawled out of the hedge and stood up.

Calm down, Anna. Breathe. Breathe.

He scanned his surroundings and then walked a few paces out into the field. His pack was strapped to his back.

Breathe, Anna. Take a deep breath.

He had a slight limp, but that was all. So he'd been lying to us when he said his ankle was no better. What idiots we were. Why hadn't we suspected that?

He shaded his eyes from the sun and turned slowly, as though trying to get a sense of his surroundings. He stopped and looked for a long time in the direction of Ashcombe House, which was clearly visible across the fields.

Think, Anna. Calm down and think.

He thought he was in Muddle Green, didn't he? He must be going to meet his associates. Except he wouldn't meet them, because they really were in Muddle Green. But Peter Smith was one field away from an encampment of soldiers at Ashcombe Park.

Was he carrying explosives in that rucksack?

Think, Anna. Breathe and think.

I could run for help, but I was at least half a kilometre from the Park and half a kilometre from the Deans' house. By the time I'd run to either place, found somebody and told them where he was, he might be somewhere completely different. And it might be too late to stop him from doing whatever he was planning to do.

Think.

I would have to follow him. If he did go towards the Park, then surely there would be soldiers around and I could alert them.

And if I couldn't do that, I would somehow have to stop him myself.

Breathe, Anna. Breathe.

He walked back to the hedge and crawled into the gap.

I looked at the dense hedgerow in front of me. I would never catch him up if I tried to crawl through it from here. I would have to creep around the outside until I got to a point where I could keep an eye on him without him hearing or seeing me.

I left Aunty Rose's basket on the verge, just outside the gateway. It would be a sign for anyone if they came looking for me. I hid the shopping in the hedge and stuffed the precious ration books in my trouser pockets. Then I set off around the outside of the hedgerow.

What if he heard or saw me? Once I was in the middle of the hedge, I would be trapped. He could shoot me without any trouble at all.

Breathe, Anna, breathe. Calm down. Think.

He wouldn't shoot me. The noise would bring people running and he would be cornered.

He could kill me in other, noiseless ways, though, couldn't he? He could strangle me or smother me. Stuck in a hedge, I'd be powerless to escape.

Calm down, Anna. Breathe.

He was a lot bigger than I was. So if I followed the trail he had made through the hedge, I should be able to move without breaking any more twigs. The breeze rustling the leaves should mask any accidental sound I made.

I reached the gap in the hedge.

Before I crawled in, I scuffed up the ground around the gap with the soles of my shoes, creating a patch of bare soil that stood out among the green grass and leaves. If a search party looked here, they would surely notice that. I made shoe prints in the soil too. Then I got down on my hands and knees and started crawling through the hedgerow.

I followed the trail of snapped twigs that the man had left. My clothes kept getting caught on thorns and I had to stop to disentangle them. The same thing must be happening to him, I thought, only much more so. I was following a ready-made trail, but he was having to create it. His progress must be pretty slow.

I was nearly at the far corner of the field now. My hands and knees were sore from crawling on stones and twigs. Thank goodness I was wearing trousers.

I came to the end of the field, where the farm

hedge met the huge ancient yew hedge that bordered Ashcombe Park. Which direction had the man taken?

To the right, the hedge ran parallel to the tree-lined avenue all the way down to the main entrance gates. To the left, it ran up to the stable yard. If he and his associates were planning to attack the house, he would be heading left.

I squeezed through the gap where the man had broken through.

I was expecting to have to struggle through densely woven yew, but, to my amazement, when I reached the middle of the hedge, I found myself in a natural tunnel, where the centuries-old growth at the centre had died away, leaving green walls on either side. The tunnel was so high that I could stand up in it.

To the right, the ground looked untouched. But on the left I saw faint boot prints in the dusty soil.

My stomach turned over. So the man was heading up to the house. What was he planning to do? What had he already done to the soldier on guard outside the barn?

Stay calm, Anna. Breathe.

Asking pointless questions wouldn't help anyone. Forcing myself to take deep breaths, I moved through the tunnel as lightly as I could, scanning the path ahead of me all the time.

My heartbeat sped up as another sound rose above the rustling of the leaves. Marching boots, stamping on a hard surface. Shouted orders.

It's all right, I told myself, closing my eyes and taking a deep breath. *It's just the soldiers doing their drill in the stable yard.*

The stable yard. So I must be close to the house.

I opened my eyes. I gasped. I almost screamed, but I stopped myself just in time.

There he was. About fifteen metres ahead. He had his back to me. He stood completely still, not moving a muscle.

I froze, my heart hammering. If he turned, that would be it. There was nothing I could do.

He remained motionless. Was he listening for something? Waiting for something?

The soldiers were silent. An officer shouted a command. Massed boots stamped on the cobbles.

The man sprang to life. In one swift movement he turned and, with his hands shielding his face, barged his way through the right-hand side of the hedge.

Where was he going?

I had no choice. I had to follow him.

I tiptoed to the place where he had broken out of the hedge. I parted the leaves to see where he was.

I stared, confused. Less than a metre in front of me was a high brick wall.

Think, Anna.

It must be the back wall of the stables. A narrow path, just wide enough for one person, ran between the hedge and the wall.

I pushed my head a little way out of the hedge, enough to look along the path in both directions. I didn't have to worry about being heard, now we were so close to the marching soldiers, but I was terrified of being seen.

There was no sign of him. I would have to step out.

Sick with terror, I pushed my way out and stood on the earth path, flattening my body into the hedge behind me. I looked to the right. Nothing. I looked to the left.

My heart stopped.

In a small open window halfway up the wall, a pair of legs, wearing army boots and khaki trousers, dangled from the ledge.

The legs drew up. The boots planted themselves on the window ledge. They balanced there for a few seconds, and then they disappeared inside the stable.

What was he going to do?

There was no time to think. All I knew was that I had to stop him from doing something terrible.

CHAPTER FORTY-FIVE

"What to Do – and How to Do It"

If the Invader Comes

I tiptoed down the path until I was standing underneath the little window. There were other windows, but this was the only open one. A brick ledge jutted out from the wall about half a metre from the ground. By balancing on this, I could reach up to grip the window ledge. I hauled myself up, using the gaps in the crumbling mortar as footholds, until my top half was inside the stable, with my stomach resting on the window ledge and my legs dangling down the wall outside.

I scanned the dim interior. Wooden partitions separated the stalls. A couple of bulging sacks stood in the far corner, but they weren't big enough for a man to hide in. Next to them stood an empty wheelbarrow, a shovel and a pitchfork. The floor was bare apart from a heap of straw in the corner of each stall.

I stared in dread at the pile of straw beneath me. Was he hiding in there? If I jumped down, would he shoot out an arm and grab my leg?

Even if he wasn't there, he must be somewhere in these shadowy stables. And once I was inside, I would be trapped.

I screwed up my courage. The marching boots in the stable yard were so loud that I would be able to jump down without being heard. I scrabbled up to a kneeling position on the window ledge and contorted myself to pull one foot and then the other over the ledge.

Sick with fear, I jumped as lightly as I could on to the heap of straw.

Nothing moved.

The sound of marching and drilling was even louder from in here, but the doors that led to the yard were shut, so the soldiers weren't visible.

I noticed a ladder propped up against the wall in the corner to my left.

My stomach plummeted. The ladder wasn't propped against the wall. It was propped against a narrow platform just below the top of the wall, made of wooden planks. The platform ran all around the stable block.

Had the man climbed up to that platform? And had he seen me come in? Heart pounding, I tiptoed to the ladder and climbed up.

And there he was, on the other side of the platform.

He had his back to me. He was kneeling in front of a little window just under the roof. The glass was too grimy to see out into the stable yard.

He was trying to prise the window open, tugging and wriggling the rusty catch. His backpack lay beside him. He didn't seem to know I was here.

On my hands and knees, I crept along the

platform towards him. The sloping roof meant it was impossible to stand up.

"*Ja!*"

I jumped in shock. He had managed to loosen the catch. He pushed at the window but it wouldn't open. He took a penknife from his pocket, opened the blade and ran it around the window frame.

He put the knife down and pushed the window frame. This time, it opened.

He reached into his backpack and slowly drew something out.

A rifle.

He raised the rifle and pointed the barrel out of the window, aiming it into the yard below.

"No!"

He swung round, pulling the gun back through the window. As he saw me, panic and disbelief flashed across his face. My heart hammered horribly, but there was one clear thought in my head. I had to keep him talking. I had to stop him from shooting anybody.

"I went to the barn to bring you food, but you'd gone," I said. My voice came out high and strained. I took a breath.

"I was worried in case you'd been caught. So I went to the field and I saw you in the hedge and I decided to follow you in case you needed any help to get away. With your leg being bad and everything."

How stupid that sounded.

"My ankle is much better," he said. His face was strained and tense. "You must go home. I need to go to my mother's house alone."

I saw an opportunity. I attempted a broad, friendly smile. "But you're going in the wrong direction. Whitstable is the other way. Come on. I'll show you. I'll take you to the bus stop."

A flash of anger passed across his face. He seemed to be fighting to keep his features under control.

"There is something I need to do here first," he said. "You go home now."

My heart thudded against my ribs. I forced another smile.

"That's all right. I'll wait."

"I said you must leave," he spat, not bothering to conceal his impatience any more. "That is an order."

I was shaking now.

"I'm not leaving," I said.

He looked at me for a moment. Then he picked up his rifle and raised the barrel until it was pointed directly at me.

"Then I shall have to shoot you."

He smiled a horrible smile. "But first I should thank you and your friends for giving me such valuable information. If it were not for you, I should not know that Winston Churchill is coming to this very place today."

I was shaking all over. I tried to focus on his face and not the barrel of his gun.

"And what is the first thing that Mr Churchill does when he arrives at an army camp?" he said. "You know that, little girl? Shall I tell you?"

Through the overwhelming fear that flooded me,

one clear thought rose to the surface. As long as he's talking, I thought, as long as he keeps talking to me, then he won't shoot me.

"I will tell you what is the first thing he does," he said. "He inspects the troops. Why do you think all those soldiers are lined up out there, in the yard, practising their drills? It is so that the great Mr Churchill can ride up in his big shiny open car and inspect them. And when he arrives in this yard, what do you think I shall do then, little girl?"

I was cold all over. I knew exactly what he was planning to do.

He laughed. "You know, don't you? Yes, of course you do. The great British Prime Minister will be shot dead, for the glory of the *Führer* and the honour of the Third Reich."

All of a sudden, I felt strangely calm and logical.

"If you're waiting here to shoot Mr Churchill," I said, "then you can't shoot me first. There are hundreds of soldiers only a few metres away from us. They would all hear the gunshot, and you would be caught immediately. And then you would never get your chance to kill him."

"Attention!"

The command was bellowed out. A thousand boots stamped in unison, and then there was silence. A huge, echoing silence, as though everybody was waiting for something to fill it.

The man lowered his gun. But he didn't look defeated. Far from it. There was a malicious gleam in his eye and a chilling smile playing at the corners of his mouth.

"You are right," he murmured. "I cannot shoot you. But there are other ways to kill a person. Silent ways to kill little Jewish girls like you."

I looked at the sadistic smile on his face, and all my anger, all the hatred I had ever felt for Hitler and his vile gangs of thugs, all my fears for my parents, exploded into one giant ball of blind rage. With a cry of fury, I sprang at the man, swinging my right arm back to punch him in the face.

Dropping the gun, he grabbed my arm and clamped his other hand over my mouth to silence me. I saw my chance. With my left hand, I snatched up his rifle and threw it out of the window.

Shouts shattered the silence of the stable yard. The man turned white. He sprang to his feet. His head thudded against a roof beam. He yelled in pain and fell to his knees, clutching his head and letting out a stream of German swear words. Still clutching his head, he stumbled along the platform and started to scrabble down the ladder.

Doors swung open and the stable block was flooded with light. Soldiers burst in, bayonets gleaming from their guns. The man bolted for the open window where he had come in, but he hadn't run more than two steps before he was grabbed by two soldiers.

As he was marched out of the door, his arms pinned behind his back, he looked up directly into my eyes.

"*Heil Hitler!*" he shouted.

I was trembling uncontrollably. I huddled on the

platform, unable to move. A man's voice called, "Anybody there? Show yourselves!" but my voice wouldn't work.

Soldiers searched the stables, poking their bayonets into the straw. I knew I should make myself known to them, but I couldn't speak.

Then I heard a shout. "There's a girl up there!"

A soldier pointed at me. Every head turned in my direction. Another soldier raced up the ladder and crouched beside me.

"Are you all right? Did he hurt you?"

I shook my head. My teeth were chattering.

"Thank God for that," he said. "Is there anyone else here? Did you see any other men?"

I shook my head again.

"What were you doing here? Were you playing in the loft? Or did he take you hostage?"

His questions felt like an attack. I didn't know what to say.

"She's in shock, Hewitt," said a man from below. "Bring her down, for God's sake."

"Yes, sir," said the soldier. He moved to the ladder. "Now," he said to me, "I'm just going to put you over my shoulder and take you down this ladder."

Then I heard a voice I recognised.

"Found anything, lieutenant?"

"We've found a girl, sir," said the same man from below.

"A girl?"

"Yes, sir. Up on that platform, sir. Hewitt's bringing her down. Here she is, sir."

The soldier called Hewitt reached the ground, lifted me off his shoulder and sat me on a hay bale. Colonel Ferguson crouched next to me.

"Anna!" he said. "Are you all right? What did he do to you?"

With a huge effort, I managed to speak in a thin, weak voice.

"He was going to shoot Mr Churchill, so I threw his gun out of the window."

He stared at me, open-mouthed.

"What about the other men?" I said. "Did you catch them?"

"We certainly did. They were all arrested as they left their various lodgings for Muddle Green this morning. All three of them were carrying explosives. But we had no idea your man was planning a lone sniper attack. He didn't mention that in his letters. He'd told his associates he couldn't move because of his sprained ankle."

"He was lying," I said.

"We only discovered he'd escaped a few minutes ago," said the colonel. "The duty soldier went to relieve his colleague and found him bound and gagged in a corner of the barn. Your man had hit him over the head and tied him up. We were about to begin a search when that rifle fell from the sky. I suppose he couldn't resist the thought of being a lone hero. Imagine Hitler's joy if one of his spies killed the British Prime Minister."

"For the glory of the *Führer* and the Third Reich," I murmured, remembering his words.

"Are you all right, Anna?" asked the colonel. "You're terribly pale."

"Is Mr Churchill still coming?" I asked.

"Any minute now. First things first though. You don't look at all well. We need to get you home."

CHAPTER FORTY-SIX

An Invitation

Aunty Rose told me afterwards that she had been astonished when a smartly suited woman in a shiny car drove up to the cottage with her foster daughter in the passenger seat.

"Good morning, Mrs Dean," Miss Johnson said, holding out her hand. "I'm Pamela Johnson. I'm a stenographer based at Ashcombe House."

"Anna, you're so pale!" Aunty Rose said. "What's happened? Where have you been?"

"I'm afraid that Anna is not at liberty to tell you, Mrs Dean," said Miss Johnson. "Suffice it to say that she has been extremely brave and you can be very proud of her."

When Miss Johnson left, Aunty Rose took my hands in hers and gasped. "You're frozen! And you're trembling all over. Molly, love, go and put the kettle on. She needs a cup of hot sweet tea. Frank, fetch a blanket."

I saw and heard everything that was going on around me, but it was as though I were watching a play and all of this was happening to somebody else. I felt completely numb. Aunty Rose led me to the sofa and tucked a blanket around me. I drank the tea, but when she suggested I go up to bed, I found my legs were too weak to stand. She had to help me to the bedroom, where she tucked me into bed with two hot-water bottles and extra blankets.

I fell asleep instantly, but my sleep was punctured by hideous dreams. I saw my parents taken away by storm troopers, beaten and thrown into terrible prison camps. Their agonised, contorted faces filled my nightmare landscape, begging me to help them. And all the time I stood there, useless, doing nothing.

I woke up drenched in sweat again. The sounds of a house in the full hustle and bustle of the working day seeped into my consciousness. In the kitchen, crockery clattered and cutlery clinked. Oil hissed in the frying pan. I heard Aunty Rose's voice, and Molly's in reply. I smelled the sweetness of stewed fruit, mixed now with the rich scent of frying meat. I opened my eyes. The room was filled with sunshine and a vase of sweet peas stood on the bedside table.

I tried to feel relief, as it gradually sank in that the horror had just been a bad dream. But questions sneaked into my head like poisonous snakes. *How do you know it was just a bad dream? What if those things are really happening to Papa and Mama right now?*

I buried the questions in the locked box inside my head.

There was something else too, though, wasn't there? Something that nagged at the back of my mind. Something that really had happened.

And then the images began to form in my head. The rifle barrel pointed between my eyes. The harsh, mirthless laughter of the man when he revealed what he was about to do. His sadistic smile as he told me there were other, silent deaths available for Jewish girls like me.

My body jerked in a violent shudder. I burrowed down beneath the blankets until there was no light left.

When I woke again, it was dark. My head wasn't under the bedclothes any more. I heard somebody moving about in the room. When my eyes got used to the gloom, I saw it was Aunty Rose.

She must have sensed I was awake, because she turned and smiled at me. I tried to smile back. She sat on the edge of the bed and gently stroked my hair.

"How are you feeling?"

I said nothing. What could I say?

"Sorry," said Aunty Rose. "Silly question. You've only just woken up, and you've been asleep since yesterday afternoon."

She sat in silence for a while. Then she asked, "Are you hungry? Would you like something to eat or drink?"

I shook my head. After another couple of minutes, she said, "Is there anything you want to talk about? Would it help to tell me anything?"

I shook my head again. My head was full. My heart was full. But there was too much to be able to tell anybody. I would have no idea where to start. And if I did start, I was frightened I would never be able to stop. Frightened that the memories and feelings and fears might overwhelm me completely, until I drowned in them.

When Aunty Rose went back downstairs, I felt completely exhausted, but I was afraid to sleep because of the nightmares. I tried to keep my eyes open, but my eyelids were too heavy and I fell asleep again.

The next few days felt both unreal and far too real. Often I would cry out in my nightmares and would wake to find Mrs Dean or Molly at my bedside, stroking my back or head and trying to comfort me. For a blissful moment, I would feel relief. And then the relief would be swamped by terror, as the questions slithered out of the cracks in the locked box and into my conscious mind.

What if these nightmares weren't just dreams, but premonitions?

And every time, I would stuff the questions back into the box.

I had no idea what day it was any more. I lived in a trance-like state, randomly sleeping, waking and dreaming.

Then one day I woke feeling absolutely ravenous. Aunty Rose was thrilled when I walked shakily down the stairs and said I was hungry. She immediately went to work preparing a feast of eggs, fried tomatoes and toast. While she cooked, she filled me in on the progress of the war. The RAF was destroying Hitler's Luftwaffe every day, she said, in the skies right above us.

"There've been some terrific dogfights. Frank's been beside himself with excitement. We couldn't believe you slept through it all. I was in a terrible stew the first few times over whether to wake you and make you come to the shelter, but I asked the doctor and he said it was better to let you sleep. In any case, everybody round here ignores the sirens these days. Bert's been helping with the haymaking, and they all just put their steel helmets on and carry on working. As long as somebody's holding the horses, that's all they're worried about."

I felt strength flowing back into me with every mouthful of breakfast. The RAF was destroying the Luftwaffe! Perhaps everything would be all right. Perhaps Britain really would win the war and my parents could come to live in England after all.

"Molly's gone to the village on some errands, and Frank's in the woods with his friends," said Aunty Rose. "They'll be so happy to see you up and about again. They've been ever so worried. That Miss Johnson will be pleased to hear you're better too. She's been calling in every day to see how you are."

I was amazed. "Has she?"

"She brought you a letter too. I'll fetch it in a minute. She said it's an invitation to tea at Ashcombe House. Molly and Frank too, apparently." She shot me a curious look. "What have you three done to get yourselves invited to tea at Ashcombe House?

I asked those two about it but they wouldn't say a word."

"I took Colonel Ferguson some eggs," I said. "He must have really liked them."

CHAPTER FORTY-SEVEN

An Unexpected Meeting

On the following Saturday afternoon, Molly and I found ourselves sitting in the deep leather armchairs on either side of a crackling log fire in Colonel Ferguson's room. Frank was perched on a stool by the hearth. Miss Johnson was there too, not taking notes this time, but sitting on a dining chair that had been drawn up next to the armchairs. On a little table by the fire was a cake stand filled with mouth-watering biscuits and buns. The colonel and Miss Johnson must have used up all their sugar coupons for this.

"I know it's not really the weather for a fire," Colonel Ferguson said, "but Miss Johnson said you'd been in rather a state of shock, Anna, and the best cure for shock that I know of is a good strong cup of tea, plenty of cakes and proper toast made on the fire."

He went into the inner office and returned with a loaf of bread on a wooden board. He sawed the bread into slices, took a brass fork with a very long handle from a hook by the fireplace, speared a slice of bread on the fork and held it close to the flames.

I had never seen toast made on an open fire before and I watched, fascinated, as the bread turned golden. Colonel Ferguson inspected it, pronounced it satisfactory, took it off the fork and turned it around.

"I think you deserve the first slice, Miss Schlesinger," he said, when the other side was done. He buttered it, put it on a plate and held it out to me. He must have been saving all his butter ration too.

"Thank you," I said. I put the plate on my lap, aware that nobody else was eating yet.

"Well, don't be polite, girl. Eat it while it's hot."

He stuck another slice of bread on the fork. "Next one's for you, Miss Dean."

I took a bite of my toast. It was the most delicious thing I had ever eaten. The creamy saltiness of the butter melting into the crunchy surface of the toast, with its slight hint of wood smoke, and then the soft sponginess of the bread between the crunchy surfaces – it was the taste of paradise.

It wasn't until we'd finished the wonderful tea that Molly asked the question she'd been wondering about all week.

"Colonel Ferguson, are you going to tell us what's happened to the man?"

There was a knock at the door.

"Come in," called the colonel.

The door opened and Mr Rivers came in. He flashed a broad smile at us. It was the first time I'd seen him properly smile.

"Good afternoon, Anna. How nice to see you again. And you must be Molly and Frank."

They stood up, and Mr Rivers shook their hands. "Very pleased to meet you," he said. "I hear you did an excellent job of fooling our man."

Molly beamed, but Frank went bright red and shifted his eyes to the carpet.

"Don't look so mortified," said Mr Rivers. "You did a foolish thing by repeating sensitive information, but you more than made up for it by your actions afterwards."

Frank glanced at him, as if to check that he meant what he said. He seemed reassured.

"Thank you, sir," he mumbled.

Colonel Ferguson looked up from his toast. "Miss Dean was wondering what's happened to Peter Smith since last Saturday."

Mr Rivers gave Molly a very serious look. "His real name is Gerhard Hoffmann. He was one of the most dangerous and ruthless Nazi spies operating in Britain. He planned to bomb this encampment and then, when he learned that the Prime Minister was coming to inspect the troops, he planned to kill him, too. He would have had no hesitation in killing you, Anna, and frankly I'm amazed that he didn't. The fact that you managed to stop him from killing both you and the Prime Minister is a testament to your incredible bravery and presence of mind."

"I wasn't brave," I said. "It just happened."

"No," said Mr Rivers. "You made it happen. Your courageous actions saved Mr Churchill's life. The courageous actions of all three of you, in acting as go-betweens for Hoffmann's coded communications, feeding him false information and playing your parts so perfectly that he didn't suspect a thing, meant we were able to round up the whole spy ring before they could wreak any of the havoc they intended. Your actions have been exemplary. I only wish we could reward you properly, but, of course, I need hardly remind you that not a word of these events must ever be mentioned to anybody outside this room. That is of the utmost importance." His eyes met all of ours in turn. "But I think you've realised by now the dangers of repeating national secrets."

"Of course," said Molly. "But what's going to happen to the man?"

Mr Rivers' face was unreadable. "You can leave that to us. Rest assured, he will be doing no more damage."

There was another knock at the door. The colonel and Mr Rivers exchanged glances.

"Come in," said the colonel.

A soldier stepped into the room and saluted. "Your guest has arrived, sir."

"Thank you," said the colonel.

The soldier left and the colonel turned to us.

"There is somebody here who would like to meet you, Anna. Would you all mind coming with me?"

With puzzled glances at each other, we brushed the crumbs off our laps and followed Colonel Ferguson along miles of wide, carpeted corridors. Mr Rivers brought up the rear.

We were led down a grand sweeping staircase, to what I recognised as the huge entrance hall where Molly and I had first stood almost a year ago. Outside one of the many doors that led off this hall, two armed soldiers stood on guard. They saluted to the colonel, then one of them rapped smartly on the door and we were ushered into a large, elegant drawing room.

"Colonel Ferguson, Mr Stanford Rivers, Miss Anna Schlesinger, Miss Molly Dean and Master Frank Dean," the soldier announced.

A man got up from a sofa at the other end of the room. The hairs stood up on my arms. Molly gasped and Frank let out a little squeal.

Walking towards us was Winston Churchill, the Prime Minister of Great Britain. I stared at him, trying to take in the fact that I was face to face with the man whose features I knew so well from countless newspaper pictures. The man the world was relying on to save us from Hitler.

He wore a pin-striped suit with a spotty bow tie, and a gold watch chain looped across his waistcoat. As he looked at us, his serious face, with the deep frown line between his eyebrows, broke into a smile that transformed him from a bulldog to a cheeky schoolboy.

He surveyed us with twinkling eyes. "So," he said, "which one of you is Anna?"

To hear that voice, so familiar from his amazing speeches on the wireless, gave me goose pimples.

I couldn't speak.

"That's Anna," said Molly, gesturing to me. "She followed the man up to the stable loft and knocked his rifle into the yard."

Mr Churchill fixed his gaze on me and held out his hand. Dazed, I held out mine. He shook it vigorously.

"Anna Schlesinger," he said. "It is a very great honour to meet you."

Then he shook Molly and Frank's hands. "I've been told that you acted with great courage and presence of mind. Very well done, both of you. Very well done indeed."

He turned back to me. "I gather that you came to England as a refugee from the Nazis, Anna?"

"Yes, sir," I managed to say.

"Then it must have taken even greater reserves of courage for you to face a Nazi spy. You should be extremely proud of yourself."

"Thank you, sir," I said.

Mr Rivers gave us each a hearty handshake before Miss Johnson drove us home. Frank and Molly got into the car first. As I was about to get in, Mr Rivers took a silver card case from his inside jacket pocket, opened it and handed me a little card. On it was printed the name "Stanford Rivers Esq.", a London address and a telephone number.

"Once you're twenty-one," he said, "if you'd like a job, just drop me a line."

"Twenty-one? But that's eight years away."

"I'm afraid there's nothing I can do about that,"

he said with a completely straight face. "I'm sure you know perfectly well that the Secret Service doesn't employ children."

CHAPTER FORTY-EIGHT

Afterwards

I wish that was the end of the story. I wish I could finish it there, in that beautiful drawing room at Ashcombe House, the day we met Winston Churchill and the Secret Service offered me a job.

But it didn't end there, of course. Life at the Deans' house carried on, as normally as it could with the war raging in the air all around us. School started again in the autumn, with lots more evacuees from London now that the Germans were bombing the city almost every night. Occasionally I got taunted for being German: some of those children couldn't, or wouldn't, believe that not all Germans were Nazis. I told Molly to ignore the taunts, but she always leapt to my defence, and there were huge fights in the playground. I kept out of them. There was enough violence in the world without me adding to it.

There was only one time I retaliated. On the first day of the autumn term, Billy Townsend came up to me on the school field.

"I've got my eye on you, Anna Schlesinger," he said in what he clearly hoped was a menacing tone. "Everyone else might be fooled by you, but I'm not.

I know you're really a spy."

I looked at his freckled schoolboy face and I burst out laughing. After what I'd been through that summer, the idea that Billy Townsend could scare me was hilarious.

Billy flushed bright red. He looked embarrassed and furious. He turned to walk away.

"Maybe I am a spy, Billy," I called after him. "But if I am, then I'm hardly likely to tell you, am I? And if I'm any good at it, then you'll never find out whether I am or not, will you?"

Anyway, neither Molly nor I spent much longer at the village school. Miss Marshall managed to persuade Aunty Rose that we should both sit for the scholarship exams at the girls' grammar school in the nearby town. We were absolutely thrilled when we both won scholarships.

Aunty Rose wasn't quite so thrilled. She was worried about not being able to afford the books and uniforms.

"Don't worry," I said. "I'll write a letter."

She assumed I was writing to Bloomsbury House, but I had a better idea. I knew the Refugee Children's Movement didn't have much money and, in any case, even if they agreed to pay for my uniform, they certainly wouldn't be able to pay for Molly's. So I got out the little card Mr Rivers had given me and sat down to write to him.

A few days later I received a cheque in the post, enough to buy uniforms for both of us, plus all the books we would need. Aunty Rose was amazed by the generosity of the Refugee Children's Movement.

It was about this time that I decided I wanted to become a doctor. I wanted to be able to save lives, to heal people, to be a positive force in the world. It seemed obvious to me that, with so many people determined to destroy life, the destructive people needed to be outnumbered by people who could make things better.

I kept this ambition to myself. I worried that if I told anybody, they would laugh at me, or think I was being big-headed to dare to imagine that I might be able to study medicine at university. But my secret dream was a constant incentive to work hard and make the most of the opportunity I'd been given. And how proud my parents would be!

My first thought every morning and my last thought every evening was of my parents, and what might be happening to them now. When they stopped answering my Red Cross letters, early in 1942, I managed to convince my waking brain that they had gone into hiding and were safe in a friend's attic or cellar somewhere. My sleeping brain wasn't convinced though, and there were many nights when I woke from a nightmare drenched in sweat, my heart hammering and a sick feeling in the pit of my stomach.

In June 1944, Allied troops finally invaded occupied France in the D-Day landings and fought their way across Europe to overthrow the Nazi regime for good. And then came the worst thing of all. As city after city fell to the Allies, the concentration camps were liberated and we finally began to learn the full truth of what the Nazis had done to the Jews.

Reports of unbelievable horrors started coming in. I forced myself to listen and read about it, but I could not allow myself to think my parents might have suffered like that. They must have managed to hide or escape. They must have survived.

I threw myself into my schoolwork. I worked non-stop, so that I had no time to think about anything else. I was in the Sixth Form now. The headmistress took a group of us who were hoping to go to the university on a day trip to Cambridge. For me, it was love at first sight. The ancient colleges with their perfect green lawns; the students on their bicycles, like scholarly crows with their black gowns flapping behind them and their bicycle baskets heaped with books; the beautiful river with the weeping willows trailing their branches in the water: it seemed to me the epitome of culture and civilisation.

From that day forward, my one ambition was to win a scholarship to study medicine at this magical place. And, unlike the desperate hope that my parents had survived the war, this was an ambition I had some control over.

After the Germans finally surrendered, in May 1945, we wrote to every organisation that might have information, but they had no news of my parents. We waited and waited for news. I pestered Bloomsbury House, but their enquiries produced no results. I wrote to our old neighbours and friends in Germany, everyone whose address I could remember.

I received no replies.

And then, one day in January 1946, a letter arrived from Switzerland. It was from my Uncle Paul. He told me that both my parents had died in Auschwitz concentration camp, my father in 1943 and my mother just before the end of the war.

CHAPTER FORTY-NINE

Back to the Present

Tears filled my grandmother's eyes. She pulled a tissue from the sleeve of her cardigan and dabbed them away.

"I'm sorry, Daniel," she said. "It brought it all back."

I leaned across and squeezed her hand. Mum had told me that Granny's parents died in the war, but hearing it from her, and knowing everything else that had happened, was still a shock.

She smiled at me through her tears.

"I think I might need a little sleep now. Do you mind, darling? Come back tomorrow and I'll tell you anything else you want to know."

When I went back the next day, Granny was her usual cheerful self again. She gave me a big hug and took me out to the sunny garden, where she had already set the teapot and a huge plate of biscuits on the table. The framed black-and-white photo of her parents was there too.

"It's all such a long time ago now," she said, once she had poured the tea and settled herself in her chair. "But it's funny. The older I get, the more I find myself thinking about my childhood. It seems more and more important, somehow. Everything that's happened in my life has been shaped by those first twelve years. I think about my parents every single day."

She glanced at the photo, still in amazingly good condition considering it was almost eighty years old.

"That picture and their letters are all I have of them. They're my most treasured possessions." She smiled at me. "I talk to them every day, you know. I did that during the war and I never lost the habit."

"Can I ask you something?" I asked.

"Of course."

"Your Uncle Paul – what happened to him after the war? Did you see him again?"

Inka came out from the house and jumped on to Granny's lap. Granny poured herself another cup of tea and stroked the cat as she spoke.

"After I heard about my parents, I spent months consumed with grief. I had always made myself believe we would be reunited after the war, and now all my hopes had been destroyed. The future seemed utterly bleak and life didn't seem worth living. I realised I was completely alone in the world and I didn't know how to cope with that.

"Uncle Bert and Aunty Rose were wonderful, of course. They said they would always be my family. They even offered to adopt me, but I wasn't ready for that. I loved them, but I wanted *my* family. And I needed time to grieve.

"The Deans were so kind and generous. And they understood, somehow, even before I did, that I needed to be reunited with Uncle Paul. He was my only living relative now. They dealt with all the paperwork and they managed to get permission for him to come and live with us in England."

"How did you all fit in?" I asked, thinking of the tiny two-bedroom cottage that Granny had painted such a vivid picture of in my mind.

She smiled. "You may well ask! We happened to have a spell of lovely weather when Uncle Paul arrived, so Molly and I slept in a tent in the garden and he had our room. We loved sleeping outdoors – in fact, some nights, we didn't sleep in the tent at all, just on a groundsheet under the stars. We would lie on our backs and look up at the night sky, and I would imagine my parents up there, watching over me."

I didn't quite know how to ask the next question. "And your Uncle Paul? Was he... Was he all right?"

Granny gazed into the distance for a minute before she spoke.

"He was very different. He had spent two years in a concentration camp, and it was an old man who came shuffling up to me at Liverpool Street Station. I didn't even recognise him. He seemed so much smaller than before. His hair was completely white and he was so thin and stooped. He looked as though a breeze would blow him over. But his eyes lit up when he saw me, and suddenly I realised who he was."

"Did he get better?" I asked, desperately hoping for a happy ending for Uncle Paul.

"Gradually, he did. It was good that the weather was so lovely when he came over. He enjoyed sitting in the garden, looking at the flowers and listening to the birdsong. He fed the birds every morning, and some of them grew so tame that they would come and sit right beside his chair. He helped around the house too, just sitting at the kitchen table peeling vegetables and that sort of thing to start with, but more and more as he got stronger – gardening and odd jobs and so on. The Deans' idea had been to find lodgings for him in the village once he got a bit better, but then they grew so fond of him that they didn't want him to move out, and they persuaded Lord Hurstwood to build an extension on the cottage so that he could stay. He lived there for the rest of his life."

She smiled. "Mind you, I lost my cat to him. He loved Clover, and she adored him. They became completely devoted to each other. She would sit in his lap in the sun all day, purring away like a steam engine while he stroked her. She had no time for me at all once Uncle Paul arrived. But it worked out well, really, because I went away to university soon afterwards, and I couldn't have taken her with me."

"So you got your place at Cambridge?"

"Yes," she said. "They offered me a place for the Michaelmas term of 1946, but I almost didn't go. I was so shaken and battered by grief that going to Cambridge didn't seem to matter any more. I told

Uncle Paul that I didn't think I should take up the place."

"Why not?" I asked, amazed.

"I think I felt guilty."

"Guilty? About what?"

"About being so lucky, perhaps. Why had I survived, when so many people had died? The Nazis murdered one and a half million Jewish children. They murdered my parents. What right did I have, not only to be alive, but to win a scholarship to study in the most beautiful place in the world?"

"But you were studying medicine. To help people."

"That's what Uncle Bert and Aunty Rose said. And I knew that, of course. But I couldn't shake the guilt."

"So what changed your mind?"

"That was Uncle Paul. It was so wonderful to have him back. You can't imagine what a help it was to have somebody there from my life before the war, somebody who was a connection to my parents."

"So how did he change your mind?"

Granny paused for a while.

"He got angry with me one day. It was the only time I ever saw him really angry. I was feeling utterly wretched about my parents. I kept torturing myself with thoughts of what they must have gone through. I couldn't stop thinking about it. I had nightmares every night, even worse than the ones I'd had during the war. One day, I was feeling at rock bottom. I couldn't stop crying. And I said to Uncle Paul that I should never have come to England. I'd abandoned my parents. I should have stayed with them and we should have died together. And he got so angry.

"'Don't ever say that again,' he said. 'If they had had to watch you suffer too, in that place, and they'd been powerless to help you...' He shuddered. 'The only happiness they had was in knowing that they had been able to save you. The only hope they had left was the hope that you would go on to live a good life.'

"'But I can never thank them. I can never repay them.'

"'Anna,' he said. 'Every letter you sent repaid them. Every communication they had from you brought them hope. The knowledge that you were happy in England, well cared for, safe – that repaid them. And you know what you should do now?'

"I shook my head. Uncle Paul took my hands and looked into my eyes.

"'Go to Cambridge. Be happy. Go out into the world and work and make a success of your life. That's what your parents would want. That's why they made that sacrifice, so that you could have a life. That is the best possible way to repay them.'"

Granny looked at me and there were tears in her eyes again. "And he was right, of course. He was completely right. From that moment on, I knew I must honour my parents' sacrifice by making my life count for something, by trying to be useful and happy, by always trying, in my own small way, to make the world a better place."

"Can I ask you one more question?"

"Of course."

"Did you ever get in touch with Mr Rivers?"

"What do you mean?" Her face, which had been so full of emotion, all at once became an unreadable mask.

"When he gave you his card that day and offered you a job when you were twenty-one. Did you get in touch with him when you were twenty-one?"

"Ah," said Granny, a smile playing at the corners of her mouth. "That would be telling. Let's just say, there are a lot more files in the vaults of MI5 that are still waiting to be declassified." And she gave me the faintest hint of a wink.

CHAPTER FIFTY

A Birthday Surprise

Granny didn't want a big fuss for her ninetieth birthday. So we didn't go anywhere fancy. Instead, we did what she liked best, which was to fill our house with all her favourite people.

There were all her children and grandchildren, of course. Granny was never happier than when her whole family was together in one room. There was her best friend, Molly, who had recently celebrated her own ninetieth birthday. She lived in Wales now, to be near her grandchildren, and she had just had a hip replacement, but she said she wouldn't miss Granny's party for the world. And there was Molly's brother, Frank, with all his children and grandchildren. Frank's son was now the carpenter on the Ashcombe estate, continuing the family tradition started by his grandfather.

There were all Granny's friends and neighbours in the village, and lots of friends from her work. To be honest, it was really lucky the weather was nice, because I don't think everyone would have fitted in the house. Granny was having a wonderful time, moving from one group to the next, everybody showering her with love and affection.

But we were still waiting for one guest. Every time I thought about his arrival, my stomach turned over with excitement and nerves. This had all been my idea, and I had arranged everything. I'd been so sure she'd be thrilled, but now, as it was about to happen, I began to have terrible doubts. What if she didn't want to be reminded of the past? What if it was too much of a shock for her?

The doorbell rang. My stomach tensed into knots.

Molly, who was in on the secret, glanced at her watch. Granny was in the middle of a conversation. Molly tapped her on the shoulder.

"That's for you, Anna."

"Who is it?" asked Granny. "I thought everybody was here."

Molly winked at her. "You'd better go and find out, hadn't you? He's come a long way to see you."

Looking confused, Granny walked down the hall to the front door. I hovered anxiously behind her. Molly squeezed my hand excitedly.

A tall, broad man with white hair and glasses stood on the doorstep, holding the biggest bunch of flowers I had ever seen.

"Anna Schlesinger?" he asked.

"Yes," said Granny, sounding puzzled. She hadn't been Anna Schlesinger for over fifty years.

"You don't recognise me, do you?" said the man.

"I'm afraid I don't. Should I?"

He smiled. "I'd be amazed if you did. I looked very different when you last saw me."

"Anna!" called Molly. "Aren't you going to invite your guest inside?"

"I'm sorry," Granny said to the man. "Could you tell me who you are?"

"Come in and sit down first," said Molly. "It's nice and quiet in the kitchen. Everyone's out in the garden."

The man gestured for Granny to lead the way. She walked through to the kitchen, shooting Molly a querying look as she passed her. Molly's face was full of suppressed excitement.

"Tea?" said Molly.

"Lovely, yes, please," said the man.

Molly went to the sink to fill the kettle. I hovered in the background. Mum saw us through the kitchen window and I beckoned for her to come in.

Granny sat down and the man sat next to her. Mum appeared in the doorway and squeezed my hand.

The man looked intently into Granny's eyes.

"I'm sorry to keep you in suspense," he said. "I'm at a distinct advantage here. I've been looking for you for years, but you've probably forgotten I ever existed."

Granny said nothing, but she suddenly looked very alert, as though she sensed that something important was happening.

"On 12th July 1939," he said, "you travelled from Germany to England on the Kindertransport. All the way to England, you looked after a baby. You fed him and changed him and comforted him.

You refused to let him be taken to an orphanage in Holland, and so, without knowing it at the time, you saved his life. You slept beside him on the boat and you handed him over to his foster carer in London."

Granny nodded. Her eyes were fixed on his face.

He reached out and took both of her hands in his.

"Anna Schlesinger," he said. "My name is Ezra Neumann. I am that baby. I owe you my life."

Later in the evening, after all the crying and the laughing and the hugging and the talking, my grandmother gave a little speech. She thanked everybody for coming and for being part of her life.

"I am so lucky," she said. "I have led such a full, happy life. And I am grateful for that life every single day, knowing how many people would have loved my opportunities and never had them. Knowing how many people today, in troubled places all over the world, don't have those opportunities.

"And finally, I want to honour four wonderful people who, sadly, are not with us any more, but whose spirits will live on forever. Firstly, my extraordinary foster parents, Bert and Rose Dean. They weren't wealthy. They didn't have spare money, or spare time, or even a spare room. But they cared about what was happening to children in a country across the sea, and they offered to take in a refugee child. Had it not been for them, I would have been one of the one and a half million children murdered by the Nazis, one of the one and a half million children who never had the chance to live their lives."

She swallowed, and then she said, "And, most of all, I want to honour my parents, Ruth and Walter Schlesinger, who gave me life twice over. Once when I was born, and a second time when they put me on a train to England, knowing it might be the last time they would ever see me. I don't know if I would ever have had the courage to make that sacrifice. But I know that I owe it to them to appreciate what I have and to remember, always, that every person in the world is equally valuable. That we all matter."

She paused. Her eyes were looking into the distance.

"When I left Germany in 1939," she said, "one of the last things my father said to me was, 'Now, whatever happens, you must always be my cheerful, brave little girl.'"

She came back to the present. She smiled at all the guests, and there was just the merest trace of tears in her eyes as she finished her speech.

"And," she said, "I think I have been."

Acknowledgements

Anna is a fictional character and the story of the man in the barn is fictional, but all Anna's other experiences, in Germany and in England, are inspired by the experiences of the children who came to England on the Kindertransport. I owe an immense debt of gratitude to all the Kinder who have given interviews and written about their experiences. For the scenes on the train, I drew particularly on the writings of and interviews with Emmy Mogilensky, including a detailed interview in the United States Holocaust Memorial Museum Oral History Archive.

Many thanks to Jackie Sullivan, archivist at Roedean School, for finding evocative documents about the Jewish refugees who came to Roedean from Nazi-occupied Europe in the 1930s.

I am enormously grateful to Emma Shevah, who sprang into action when I was trying to find somebody with in-depth knowledge of Kindertransport to read the manuscript. Emma contacted Dr Tom Haward at the UCL Holocaust Education Centre, who contacted Ruth-Anne Lenga at UCL, who contacted Janet Mills at the National Holocaust Centre. Thanks to all of you for being part of the chain of connections that led to Janet putting me in touch with Amy Williams, whose PhD focuses on how the Kindertransport has been remembered and represented around the world. I am incredibly grateful to Amy and to her lead supervisor, Professor William Niven, both of whom generously took the time to read the novel and gave me thoughtful and thought-provoking feedback. I am very grateful to Amy also for sharing with me some of her fascinating research and writing about the Kindertransport.

Thank you to Sue Durrant – our chats about writing inspired me to approach the first draft in a different way from previous books. Thank you also for reading the manuscript and giving such encouraging feedback.

I am incredibly lucky to work with the most wonderful team at Nosy Crow. Huge thanks to Catherine, Rebecca, Fiona, Hester, Karen, Beth, Erin and Lauren, who all read the manuscript at various stages and were enormously encouraging. Thanks also to Nicola Theobald for her fabulous cover design and Daniela Terrazzini for the beautiful artwork. Most of all, to my amazing editor, Kirsty Stansfield, thank you for the unflagging support and for the perfectly-expressed advice that helped me weave the different story elements together.

Thank you to my wonderful children, Freddy and Dorothea, who help to inspire everything I write. (And I'm sorry I didn't end up using your excellent title suggestions.)

And lastly, as always, infinite thanks to my husband, Oliver, for all the discussions, ideas and feedback, and most of all for the unfailing support that makes everything possible.

Author's Note

In 2017, my husband, Oliver, who is head of a secondary school, returned from the school's Founders' Day commemoration and told me about an elderly woman who had introduced herself to him after the service. Now in her nineties, she had travelled back to show her gratitude to the school that had taken her in as a Jewish refugee from Nazi-occupied Europe just before the outbreak of the Second World War. She described how her father, at the moment of parting as he put her on the train, had cut off her plaits, hoping that if she could pass as a boy then she would be safer on the journey. "I travelled all the way to England," she said, "with my pigtails in my pockets."

We were both very moved by this account, especially the bravery and sacrifice of the parents who sent their children away to safety, knowing they might never see them again, and the courage of these children as they travelled alone across Nazi-occupied Europe to start a new life with strangers.

I started to think about writing a story that would show how a young girl comes to be in a situation where she has to leave her family and travel to safety in another country. I began to research the Kindertransport, the coordinated rescue effort that brought ten thousand children, mostly Jewish, from Nazi-occupied Europe to Britain.

I watched documentaries, attended talks, listened to recorded interviews and read many memoirs of former "Kinder", as they named themselves. I also read a book called ...*And the Policeman Smiled: 10,000 Children escape from Nazi Europe*, by Barry Turner. From this book, I was surprised to discover that one of Oliver's relatives, Elaine Blond, was a leading organiser of the Kindertransport in England. From 1938-1948, Elaine Blond was a full-time volunteer with the Refugee Children's Movement at Bloomsbury House. She had, as she said, "the official title of Treasurer," but in fact "there was no such thing as job demarcation... I was available for any job that was going, from meeting the latest arrivals at the quayside to checking out prospective foster parents." After the war, she helped to organise the resettlement in England of child survivors of the concentration camps.

As I learned more about the Kinder, I was awed and moved by the courage of these children, who quickly learned English, settled into new schools and often excelled academically and then in their chosen careers. They had to find a way to deal with the constant worry about their families while forging new lives for themselves, often sustained and driven by advice their parents had given them in their final days together, as parents tried to cram a lifetime's worth of guidance into a few days or weeks.

I wanted to write a story that would engage readers and also help them to think about the experiences of children who have to leave their homes because of war or persecution. I am very aware that Anna's experience is worlds away from my own, but her story was one that interested me deeply and that I felt had something to say, not only about the frightening power of prejudice and hatred, but also the transformative power of courage and kindness. I hope I have done it justice.

Bibliography

I could not have written *Anna at War* without the following books and sources:

Kindertransport by Olga Levy Drucker (New York: Henry Holt and Company, 1992)

Pearls of Childhood by Vera Gissing (London: Robson Books Ltd, 1988)

Other People's Houses by Lore Segal (New York: Harcourt Brace Jovanovich, 1963)

The Ninth of November by Hannele Zurndorfer (London: Quartet Books Ltd, 1983)

The Children of Willesden Lane by Mona Golabek and Lee Cohen (London: Franklin Watts, 2017)

We Came as Children: A Collective Autobiography, edited by Karen Gershon (London: Victor Gollancz Ltd, 1966)

I Came Alone: The Stories of the Kindertransports, edited by Bertha Leverton and Shmuel Lowensohn (Lewes: The Book Guild Ltd, 1990)

...And the Policeman Smiled: 10,000 Children Escape from Nazi Europe, by Barry Turner (London: Bloomsbury, 1991)

Marks of Distinction: The Memoirs of Elaine

Blond, with Barry Turner (London: Valentine, Mitchell & Co. Ltd, 1988)

On Hitler's Mountain: Overcoming the Legacy of a Nazi Childhood, by Irmgard A. Hunt (New York: HarperCollins, 2005)

The Children Who Cheated the Nazis: The Complete Transcript of the TV Documentary (The Kinder Archive Project Ltd, 2012. TV documentary produced for Channel 4 by Golden Reed Productions Ltd)

Nicky's Family: The true story of the 'British Schindler', Sir Nicholas Winton, film directed by Matej Mináč, 2011

Into the Arms of Strangers: Stories of the Kindertransport, film directed by Mark Jonathon Harris (Warner Bros. Pictures, 2000)

The Nazis – A Warning from History, BBC documentary, 1997

How We Lived Then: A History of Everyday Life during the Second World War, by Norman Longmate (London: Hutchinson and Co. Ltd, 1971)

Mrs Miles's Diary: The Wartime Journal of a Housewife on the Home Front, by Constance Miles, edited by S.V. Partington (London: Simon & Schuster UK Ltd, 2013)

Jambusters: The Story of the Women's Institute in the Second World War, by Julie Summers (London: Simon & Schuster UK Ltd, 2013)

Agent Zigzag, by Ben MacIntyre (London: Bloomsbury, 2007)

Travellers in the Third Reich: The Rise of Fascism

Through the Eyes of Everyday People, by Julia Boyd
(London: Elliott & Thompson Ltd, 2017)

I also owe a huge debt of gratitude to the websites
and virtual archives of the National Archive, BBC
WW2 People's War, the United States Holocaust
Memorial Museum and the British Library.